was thrilled to help choose not only the
...ut the decorations, too. They spent half
...ternoon putting the decorations on the
...nd Stephanie lifted her up so she could
...e angel on the very top.

...done a fantastic job. Thank you so much,'
...ie said, and kissed the tip of Mia's nose.

...ed at her, then put her arms round Stephanie's
...u kissed me.'

...K?' Had she gone too far?

...ed. 'But you only kiss people you love.'

...; Mia said, and kissed the end of Stephanie's

...had a huge lump in her throat as she
..., 'I love you, too.'

...girl fell asleep on the sofa not long afterwards,
...ed out. Stephanie gently put a blanket over her.

...to get her home,' Daniel said.

...ie shook her head. 'Don't wake her just yet,
...e paused. 'Well, now I have a tree, I really ought
...a Christmas party.'

...ee of us?' he asked.

...inking...is it too late to ask your family over for
...as Eve?'

That s...
'What, ...
He smi...

Dear Reader

I rather like stories where the hero and heroine teach each other to trust again and/or love again.

My heroine doesn't think she'll ever fit into a family because she's never had one—except in-laws who didn't ever accept her for who she was. This is where my hero and his daughter come in. They need to learn to love again and open their hearts—which is what she does for them.

This idea actually started last year, when I got my twice-yearly cold. It *always* turns into a horrible croupy cough, nobody in the house gets any sleep for about a week, and I can't nag about homework because I lose my voice (that bit is popular and almost makes up for the lack of sleep). I was having a bit of a pity party on Facebook about it when one of my readers e-mailed me and suggested I got checked out for reactive airways. I looked up the condition (which I don't have, by the way—I'm just prone to croup), and thought it would be a great way for my hero and heroine to meet... (A special thank you to Pat Amsden for the lightbulb moment.)

I also love writing about Christmas. The season's one of my favourites, with its chance to spend some real quality time with my family. (And I admit I love all the sparkling lights and the special ornaments on the tree. And now my littlest is old enough she helps me find the perfect presents for her dad's and brother's stockings.) When my children were really small, one of our favourite Christmas traditions was taking them to see Santa. So I couldn't resist getting my hero and heroine to take his daughter to see Santa—and that, of course, led to finding out what she really, really wanted for Christmas...

Oh, and then there are the scallops. My daughter and I discovered them while I was writing the book, played around with different ways of cooking them, and thought it should be this book's recipe :) Enjoy!

I'm always delighted to hear from readers, so do come and visit me at www.katehardy.com

With love

Kate Hardy

HER REAL FAMILY CHRISTMAS

BY
KATE HARDY

MILLS & BOON

First published in Great Britain 2013
by Mills & Boon, an imprint of Harlequin (UK) Limited.
Harlequin (UK) Limited, Eton House,
18-24 Paradise Road, Richmond, Surrey TW9 1SR

© Pamela Brooks 2013

ISBN: 978 0 263 89923 8

Harlequin (UK) policy is to use papers that are natural, renewable and recyclable products and made from wood grown in sustainable forests. The logging and manufacturing process conform to the legal environmental regulations of the country of origin.

Printed and bound in Spain
by Blackprint CPI, Barcelona

Kate Hardy lives in Norwich, in the east of England, with her husband, two young children, one bouncy spaniel, and too many books to count! When she's not busy writing romance or researching local history she helps out at her children's schools. She also loves cooking—spot the recipes sneaked into her books! (They're also on her website, along with extracts and stories behind the books.) Writing for Mills & Boon® has been a dream come true for Kate—something she wanted to do ever since she was twelve. She's been writing Medical Romances™ for over ten years now and also writes for Mills & Boon® Romance. She says it's the best of both worlds, because she gets to learn lots of new things when she's researching the background to a book: add a touch of passion, drama and danger, a new gorgeous hero every time, and it's the perfect job!

Kate's always delighted to hear from readers, so do drop in to her website at www.katehardy.com

Recent books by Kate Hardy:

A DATE WITH THE ICE PRINCESS*
THE BROODING DOC'S REDEMPTION*
BALLROOM TO BRIDE AND GROOM**
ONCE A PLAYBOY…*
THE HIDDEN HEART OF RICO ROSSI†
DR CINDERELLA'S MIDNIGHT FLING *
THE EX WHO HIRED HER†

*In Mills & Boon® Medical Romance™
**In Mills & Boon® Romance
†In Mills & Boon® Modern™ Romance

To Pat Amsden, with thanks for the lightbulb moment.

CHAPTER ONE

'IT'S ALL RIGHT, darling.' Daniel stroked his daughter's hair, and hoped that the panic seeping through his veins didn't show in his voice. 'Don't try to talk. Just breathe. In for two, out for two. Good girl. And again. In for two, out for two.'

How could Mia have got so much worse in one short hour?

The old trick of a steamy bathroom helping to calm a child's airways wasn't working. She couldn't stop coughing; and it was a horrible, barking, croupy cough. He'd just bet that if she were wired up to a pulse oximeter, her oxygen stats would be way too low.

He had to act. Now. He needed to take her to hospital.

Should he call an ambulance? No, it'd scare her too much. And in any case he could drive her there quicker than an ambulance could get to his house and back to the hospital.

Except that meant Mia would be on her own in the back of the car, in her seat, with nobody to hold her hand and calm her down. Sure, he could call his mum or his sister and they'd come straight over to help—but that would mean waiting for them to get to his house. And right now he didn't think waiting was an option.

Not for the first time, Daniel wished he wasn't a single

dad. If that stupid, selfish elderly driver who'd mown down his wife on the footpath hadn't been so stubborn and had taken a taxi that day, instead of driving a car she really hadn't been capable of handling any more.

But wishing wasn't going to bring Meg back. It was pointless and self-indulgent, and he was only letting himself wish it now because he was panicking that he'd let his daughter down. Panicking that he'd lose his precious girl because he hadn't kept a close enough eye on her and realised how bad her symptoms were getting.

What kind of useless father was he?

What kind of useless *doctor* was he?

He scooped Mia up into his arms. 'I think,' he said softly, 'we need to get you some special medicine for that cough. And we don't have any indoors. So I need to take you to where I work, OK?'

Mia nodded, her brown eyes huge. So like Meg's. Guilt spiked through him; right now he was letting Meg down as well as Mia.

'Good girl. Let's go.' Daniel grabbed a blanket from her room on the way, along with her favourite teddy, and closed the front door behind him. 'Daddy's going to be driving so I can't hold your hand, but Fred Bear's going to give you a special cuddle for me so you don't feel lonely, OK?' He strapped her into her car seat, put Fred Bear into her arms, and arranged the blanket quickly so she wouldn't get cold.

He talked to her all the way to the hospital. All the way from scooping her out of her car seat until they got to the reception of the emergency department. And, all the way, the only thing that he could hear from her was that dreadful deep cough.

To his relief, the triage nurse saw them immediately, and sent her straight through to the paediatric assessment unit.

The doctor on duty wasn't one he knew, but that didn't matter—just as long as she treated his daughter right now.

'Hello, Mia. I'm Dr Stephanie Scott,' the doctor said, crouching down so she was at the child's height.

Mia managed the first syllable of a reply before she started coughing.

'It's OK, sweetheart, you don't have to talk,' Stephanie said. 'I can hear exactly what's wrong with you. What I'm going to do now is put a special mask on your face, which will help you breathe a bit better and not cough quite so much, and I'd also like to put a special sleeve on your finger. It won't hurt. It just shines a light through your finger and tells me some numbers that will help me to make you feel better. Is that OK?'

The little girl nodded.

Daniel knew what Stephanie Scott was checking for when she put the oximeter on Mia's finger: pulse and oxygen saturation. Good. Just what he would do.

Stephanie looked at the readings and smiled at the little girl. 'That's what I thought it would say. Mia, I'm going to give you some special medicine through another mask that will *really* help with that cough, and then I need to talk to Daddy for a little bit because I think he's going to find it easier to talk to me than you are, right now. Is that OK with you?'

At the little girl's nod, she glanced over at Daniel. 'I'm going to give her a medicine called adrenalin—it will help a lot with her breathing. And I'm going to do it through a nebuliser so all she has to do is breathe it in. It looks a lot scarier than it is, but she's going to be absolutely fine, OK?'

'OK.' Daniel was holding it together. Just. But he found himself relaxing as he watched her work. Stephanie Scott clearly knew what she was doing and she was really good with Mia, talking her through what she was doing as she hooked the little girl up to the nebuliser, and reassuring her all the while. And that smile—she had the kind of smile that lit up a room.

Daniel caught his thoughts and grimaced. What on earth was he doing, thinking about that sort of thing when his daughter was desperately ill? Especially when he hadn't been involved with anyone since Meg's death, four years ago, and had concentrated on his daughter and his job rather than his social life? Hot shame flooded through his cheeks, mingled with guilt. Right at that moment, he was at the end of his tether and his head felt as if it was going to implode under all the pressure.

'Mr Connor?' Stephanie asked.

He shook himself. 'I'm so sorry. I didn't catch what you said.'

'I was asking if Mia has any family history of asthma or any kind of allergies.'

'No, none.'

'Does Mia wheeze at all or say her chest feels tight or hurts?'

'No.'

'OK. Do you ever notice that Mia's a bit short of breath or her nostrils flare?'

Daniel realised swiftly that Stephanie was running through a list of asthma symptoms. 'No. Is that what you think it is? Asthma?'

'It's quite a strong possibility,' she said.

He shook his head. 'Mia just has a cold. They always go to her chest and she ends up with a bad cough—she had bronchiolitis when she was tiny and she was in here for a week on oxygen.'

Stephanie nodded. 'Colds are often worse for little ones after they've had RSV. And I guess seeing her here on oxygen is reminding you of that? It's tough.'

'Yes,' he admitted. It brought back all the nights when he and Meg had taken turns to sit at their tiny baby's bedside, feeding her through a nasogastric tube because the virus had left Mia too exhausted to drink normally. 'I guess I panicked a bit.'

'No, you did exactly the right thing, bringing her in,' Stephanie reassured him. 'She wasn't getting as much oxygen as I'd like, so the medication's going to help a lot. Though I'd also like to admit her overnight and keep an eye on her. So she's had a cold recently?'

'For three or four days. And yesterday it went to that croupy cough.' He sighed. 'Usually a steamy bathroom helps. I get her to drink warm blackcurrant or something like that, and keep her sitting upright on my lap.'

'Which are all exactly the right things to do to treat a cough,' Stephanie said. 'Colds are viral infections, Mr Connor, so antibiotics won't do anything to help and I won't prescribe them, but liquid paracetamol will help to keep Mia's temperature down.'

Daniel thought about telling Stephanie that he was a doctor and he was well aware of the problems with antibiotic resistance, but that wouldn't help Mia—and his daughter was a lot more important than his professional pride. 'I last gave her some of that about four hours ago, so she's due some more now anyway,' he said. 'The steamy bathroom didn't work this time.'

'Does she get many coughs like this?'

'Too many,' he admitted. 'She hates having time off school when this happens, but she gets so tired and the cough just won't stop.'

Stephanie looked thoughtful. 'Has your family doctor prescribed corticosteroids for her?'

'No.'

'It's usually a treatment for asthma, but it's also very

good for reducing inflammation in airways when children have this sort of virus. And I should explain that corticosteroids are the same kind of steroids that the body produces naturally, not the sort you associate with bodybuilders.'

Yes, it was way, way too late now to tell Stephanie Scott that he was a doctor; it would just embarrass them both. But Daniel liked the clear way she explained things. It was a pity she was on the emergency department team, as he had a feeling that she'd be good with neonates. Unless she was a locum, maybe? He'd check that when he was back on duty and, if she *was* a locum, he'd get Theo to add Stephanie to their list. She'd be a real asset to their team.

Mia's breathing started to ease as the medication did its job. Stephanie glanced at the readout on the oximeter. 'I'm happier now. She's responding nicely. Mia, I'd like you to stay here tonight just so we can make sure that cough's getting better or give you more of the special medicine if it doesn't. Daddy can stay with you if he wants to—' she looked at him '—or maybe Mia's mum might like to stay with her?'

Daniel was pretty sure that Mia's mum would be there in spirit; but, oh, how he wished she could be there in body, too. He'd had four years now of being a single parent, and it didn't get any easier. Missing Meg hadn't got much easier, either. Though, between them, Mia and his work kept him too busy to focus on how lonely he felt. He had to swallow the sudden lump in his throat. 'I'll stay with her,' he said gruffly.

Stephanie took him up to the children's ward, settled Mia in and made sure that Daniel was comfortable, then sorted out the paperwork. 'I'll see you both tomorrow before the end of my shift,' she said. 'If you need anything, just go and have a word with the nurse. If it's an emergency, then you press that button there and someone will be straight with you.'

He already knew all that. But he appreciated the way she was looking after them and it would be churlish to say anything. 'Thank you.'

'No worries.' She squeezed Mia's hand. 'You try to get some rest, sweetheart, OK?'

The little girl nodded tiredly.

'I'll see you later.'

Stephanie was almost tempted to call in and see the Connors on her break. Mia's father had looked so tired and worried. And it was unusual for a dad to be at the hospital with a child on his own; in her experience, mothers usually took over when a child was ill. Unless maybe Mia's mum wasn't well herself, or had been working a night shift. Or, given the way Mr Connor had flinched when she'd mentioned Mia's mum, maybe he was a single dad and he was worried about the fact his daughter had become ill so quickly when he was looking after her.

No. She needed to keep some professional distance. Besides, she knew better than to get involved—especially given the way her world had imploded the last time she'd got involved with someone else's medical problems. It had put her marriage on its final crash-and-burn trajectory; although it had been four years now since the divorce, it still hurt to think about the way things had gone so badly wrong. The way all her dreams had blown up in her face. The way she'd managed to lose a second family. And all because she'd put her job first.

Now her job was all she had. And that had to be enough.

She shook herself. Enough of the self-pity. She needed to concentrate on what she was supposed to be doing: working the night shift on the paediatric assessment unit.

Though her shift was reasonably quiet, and that gave her time to research her hunch on Mia Connor's condition.

When she'd done the handover at the end of her shift, she called up to the children's ward to see how Mia was getting on.

Mia's dad looked as if he'd barely slept and, although Mia was sleeping, the little girl was still coughing in her sleep.

'Hi,' he said, giving Stephanie a tired smile.

'Rough night?' she asked sympathetically.

He nodded. 'But I'm glad I could be here for her.'

'I've been thinking about Mia. Given that you don't have a family history of asthma, I think she has reactive airways. Whenever anyone gets a cold, their airways tend to get a bit swollen, but if someone has reactive airways their systems really overreact.' She drew a swift diagram on a piece of paper.

'Basically, these are Mia's lungs. They work a bit like a tree, with her windpipe as the trunk and the smaller airways like branches. The airways are covered in muscle— a bit like the bark of a tree—and inside they have mucous membranes, which produce mucus to keep the lungs clean. When she gets a cold, her muscles tighten and the mucous membranes swell and produce more mucus than usual. That makes her airways narrow, which in turn makes it harder for her to breathe.'

She glanced at him to check that he was following what she'd said; it was the clearest way she could explain things, but he obviously hadn't slept much overnight in the chair next to his daughter's bed and she wasn't sure how much of this he was taking in.

'Reactive airways.' He looked thoughtful. 'So can you give her something for it?'

'Yes. Corticosteroids, an inhaler and a nebuliser. I'll

write the prescription, but as Mia's asleep at the moment I don't want to wake her. One of my colleagues will show you how to use them when she does wake. The corticosteroids will stop the swelling in her throat, so if you get her to use the inhaler and nebuliser as soon as you spot the symptoms, hopefully she won't end up with that really croupy cough next time.'

'Thank you.'

'Though there are sometimes side effects,' Stephanie warned. 'She might have a headache or an upset tummy, or be sick. If that's the case, your family doctor can review the treatment and prescribe a slightly different medication, but this one should do the trick.'

'I appreciate that.' He raked a hand through his hair. 'And thank you for being so reassuring last night. You were really good with Mia.'

His praise warmed her—and that was dangerous. She never let herself react like this to anyone. She was good at her job and she did what needed to be done; but she didn't allow anyone too close, patient or colleague. She'd learned after Joe that she was better off on her own. Nobody to get her hopes up, and nobody to let her down.

She shrugged off his praise and gave him a small smile. 'No worries. It's what I'm supposed to do.' She wrote on Mia's chart. 'Do you have any questions, or is there anything you're not clear about with her condition and the treatment?'

'No, it's all fine. Thanks.'

'OK. Well, good luck.' She shook his hand, and left the department.

Four days later, Stephanie was called in to the maternity department to check over a baby after an emergency Caesarean section.

The obstetric surgeon was still in the middle of the operation, so Stephanie introduced herself to the midwife and the registrar and waited for the baby to be delivered.

'So what's the history?' she asked.

'The mum had pre-eclampsia—it came on really suddenly,' the midwife explained. 'She was fine at her last check-up; her blood pressure was a bit high, but she'd been rushing around all day. And then today she started feeling really rough, had a headache she couldn't shift and swollen ankles. Her community midwife sent her in to us, and her blood pressure had spiked and there was protein in her urine. Daniel wasn't happy with the baby's heartbeat and so he brought her straight up here.'

Daniel, Stephanie presumed, was the surgeon. She knew that the only cure for pre-eclampsia was to deliver the baby. 'How many weeks is she?' she asked.

'Thirty-six.'

So there was a good chance that the baby's lungs had matured enough, though the baby might still need little bit of help breathing and some oxygen treatment after the birth.

'Is there anything else I need to know?' she asked.

'That's the only complication,' the midwife said.

Though, as complications went, that one was more than enough; Stephanie was aware of all the potential problems for the baby, from low blood sugar through to patent ductus arteriosis, a problem where the blood vessel that allowed the blood to go through a baby's lungs before birth didn't close properly and caused abnormal blood flow in the heart. She'd just have to hope that the baby didn't have a really rough ride.

Once the baby was delivered and the cord was cut, Stephanie quickly checked him over. His heart rate and breathing were both a little on the low side, and his hands and feet were slightly bluish, but to her relief his muscle tone was good and he grimaced and cried. And he was a good weight, too; that would help him cope better.

She wrapped him in a clean cloth and brought him over to his mother.

'I think you deserve a cuddle after all that hard work,' she said. 'He's a beautiful boy. Now, I do want to take him up to the special care unit for a little while, because he needs a little bit of help breathing—but that's because he's a bit early and it's really common, so please don't start worrying that anything's desperately wrong. You'll be able to see him in the unit any time you like, and I'll be around if you have any questions.'

'Thank you,' the mum whispered.

By the time Stephanie had sorted out the baby's admission to the special care unit, the surgeon had finished sewing up the mum and she'd been wheeled off to the recovery room.

The surgeon came over to her, removing his mask. 'Sorry I didn't get a chance to introduce myself earlier. I'm Daniel—'

'Mr Connor,' she said as she looked up and recognised him.

He was the last person she'd expected to be here. And to think she'd been so careful to explain his daughter's condition. What an idiot she'd made of herself. As a doctor, of course he would've known the biology—especially as he was clearly senior to her, being a surgeon.

She shook herself and switched into professional mode. 'How's your little girl?'

'She's fine, thanks.' He blew out a breath. 'I feel a bit ashamed of myself now for panicking as much as I did. And I'm sorry. I really should've told you I was a doctor.'

So he felt as awkward as she did? Maybe this was salvageable, then. Which was good, because the chances were that they'd have to work together in the future. She wanted to keep all her work relationships as smooth as possible. 'It's not a problem. I think any parent panics when their child can't breathe properly, and it's probably worse when you're a doctor because you know all the potential complications—it's scary stuff.' She gave him a rueful smile. 'But I *am* sorry for drawing you that diagram. It was pretty much teaching you to suck eggs.'

He laughed. 'Don't apologise. It was a great analogy, and I needed to hear it right then. Actually, I'm glad you're on the paediatrics team. I wondered at the time if you were a locum.'

'No, I was rostered on the paediatric assessment unit. Rhys Morgan had it moved to the emergency department at about the same time that I joined the team.' She looked at him, surprised. 'Why are you pleased I'm in paediatrics?'

'Because, if you were a locum, I was going to ask Theo Petrakis—my boss—to put you on the list for Neonatal. You're good with panicky parents,' he said simply, 'and I can say that from first-hand experience.'

'Thank you.'

'Perhaps I can buy you a coffee later today?' he said.

Coffee? Was he asking her as colleague, or as a grateful parent, or as a potential date? Stephanie couldn't quite read the signals and it filled her with panic. Especially as she didn't know what his situation was. No way did she want to get in the slightest bit involved with a colleague who wasn't free.

Actually, she didn't want to get involved, full stop. Once bitten, definitely twice shy. It was safest to keep people pigeonholed as patients or colleagues, the way she'd done ever since her divorce. 'There's no need, really. I was just

doing my job.' Flustered, she added, 'I'd better get back
to my department.'

'Sure. Nice to see you again, Stephanie,' he said.

'You, too,' she said, and fled before she made even more
of an idiot of herself.

CHAPTER TWO

'STEPHANIE? YOU'VE GOT visitors,' Lynne, one of the senior paediatric nurses, said. 'They're waiting at the nurses' station for you.'

Visitors? Stephanie wasn't expecting anyone. Everyone she knew in London either worked with her or lived in the same block of flats. And Joe definitely wouldn't have come down to London to see her, to check she'd settled in OK to her new job and her new life. After the wreck of their marriage, they couldn't even be friends.

She'd walked out on him because she'd seen the blame in his eyes and his contempt for her every time he'd looked at her, and she just hadn't been able to live with it. That, and the knowledge that he was right about her. That she was a selfish woman who wouldn't know how to put a family first because she was useless at being part of a family.

Well, hey. Now wasn't the time for a pity party.

She saved the file, then headed out to the nurses' station. As she drew nearer, she recognised Daniel Connor and his daughter waiting there.

'Hello, Dr Scott,' Mia said shyly, and handed her a hand-drawn card and a paper plate covered with cling film. 'I made these for you and the nurses to say thank you for looking after me.'

Cupcakes, painstakingly decorated with buttercream and sprinkles.

Gifts from patients weren't encouraged, but a home-made card and cupcakes from a little girl were definitely acceptable. Especially as Stephanie could see that these were meant to be shared with the other staff who'd helped to look after her.

Stephanie crouched down so she was nearer Mia's level. 'Thank you very much, Mia. The card's beautiful and the cakes look lovely. Did your mummy help you make them?'

'No, Nanna Parker helped me.' There was just the tiniest wobble of her bottom lip. 'My mummy's in heaven.'

'I'm sorry,' Stephanie said softly. She'd hurt the little girl with her assumption, and she'd misjudged Daniel. He'd clearly been through the mill. She wasn't going to ask whether he'd lost his wife to illness or accident; either way would still have left a gaping hole in his and Mia's lives.

And now she understood exactly why he'd flinched when she'd asked if Mia's mum wanted to stay overnight with the little girl. It explained why he'd been so frantic about his daughter's deteriorating health, too; clearly Mia was all Daniel had left of her mother. Her heart bled for them. It would be bad enough losing someone you loved; how much worse would it be, losing someone who loved you back?

'I've still got Daddy,' Mia said, almost as if reading her mind and reminding her that life had light as well as shade.

Stephanie nodded, and looked up at Daniel. 'Sorry,' she mouthed.

He made a brief hand gesture to tell her it was OK, but she knew it wasn't. Yet again she'd messed up when it came to dealing with other people. Dealing with patients and colleagues, she could do; other kinds of personal interactions were much, much trickier. Which was why she usually managed to avoid them. Especially since the way she'd messed up with Joe and his family.

'I'd better get this young lady home,' Daniel said, as if he knew how awkward she felt and had taken pity on her.

She nodded. 'Well, thank you very much for coming in to see me, Mia. It's lovely to see that you're so much better. I'll put your card up on our special board, so everyone can see it, and we'll all really enjoy these cakes.'

'Good. I put extra sprinkles on yours,' the little girl said, pointing out one that was extra pink and sparkly.

'It looks gorgeous. Thank you.'

Stephanie waved her goodbye and shared out the cakes with the rest of the team on duty. But that evening, as she ate her cupcake, it struck her how a stranger could be so much kinder than family. And it made her feel really alone. She didn't have a family at all now, not even the in-laws who'd barely accepted her in the first place but had been the nearest she'd had to a real family. And the previous month she'd moved from Manchester to London, so she didn't have any really close friends nearby either.

She shook herself. Enough whining. Things were just fine. There was no problem at work; she'd fitted in easily to her new role and already felt part of the team. Though she knew that was probably thanks to growing up in an institution; it meant that she knew exactly how to fit in to an institution, whether it was school or university or the hospital. Whereas, when it came to family...

OK, so Joe's family had refused to accept where she'd come from and had always treated her as an outsider; but at the same time Stephanie knew she had to accept the lion's share of the blame for the wreckage of her marriage. She hadn't exactly made it easy for Joe's parents and sister, either. Not being familiar with a family dynamic, Stephanie simply didn't know how to react in a family. She'd never been quite sure what had been teasing and what hadn't; so she'd never really joined in, not wanting to get it wrong and hurt someone.

Was it any wonder they'd tended to leave her on the sidelines? And of course Joe would take their part over hers. They were his family and, despite the promises she and Joe had made in a packed church, she wasn't.

And now she was being really maudlin and pathetic. 'Stop feeling so sorry for yourself, Stephanie Scott,' she told herself fiercely. Her new life was just fine. She liked her colleagues, she liked her flat and she liked the hospital. She had a great career in the making. And she was *not* going to let a cupcake throw her. Even if it had been made with extra sparkles.

Everything was fine until the inter-departmental quiz evening on Friday night. Almost as soon as Stephanie walked into the pub and was hailed by her team, she noticed who was sitting on the maternity department's table.

Daniel Connor.

And the prickle of awareness shocked her. She wasn't used to noticing men on anything other than a patient-or-colleague basis. She hadn't been attracted to anyone since her break-up with Joe. And Daniel Connor definitely wasn't the kind of man she could let herself get attracted to. He came with complications. With baggage. *A family.* The thing she'd wanted all her life, but had learned the hard way that it just wasn't for her.

So she damped down that prickle of awareness, ramped up her smile, and threw herself into full colleague mode as she headed for the paediatric department's table.

Katrina Morgan patted the chair next to hers. 'I saved you a seat, Stephanie.'

'Thank you.' Stephanie smiled at her and slid into the seat.

'Did you do this sort of thing where you were before?' Katrina asked.

'In Manchester? Not as often as I'd have liked to,' Stephanie admitted. 'Our team nights out tended to involved Chinese food, ten-pin bowling, or going to a gig.'

'It's pretty much like that here too,' Katrina said, 'though there's the annual charity ball. My cousin helps organise that and it's the highlight of the hospital social calendar. It's a shame you'll have to wait until next year's now.'

'It's something to look forward to,' Stephanie said. Being positive. The way she'd always taught herself to be, even in those dark days before she'd walked out on her marriage. Smile with the world, and they'll all smile with you. Most of the time, anyway.

She accepted the glass of wine that Rhys Morgan offered her and thoroughly enjoyed taking part in the quiz; she'd always enjoyed trivia games. Each round, the team with the lowest score was knocked out; and the last round saw the paediatrics team going head to head with the maternity ward's team.

And the subject was history. The one subject that had almost tempted Stephanie away from doing a medical degree.

'How do you know all this stuff?' Katrina asked when Stephanie scribbled down their answers, naming Henry VIII's fourth wife and what happened to her.

'We learned a rhyme at school,' Stephanie said with a smile. 'I liked history. But I'm glad there are others in our team who know about sport. I'm hopeless when it comes to sport, and I would've lost the quiz for us.'

'You were good on literature, too,' Katrina said. 'And general knowledge.'

'Well, I read a lot.' Stephanie shrugged off the praise,

but inwardly she was pleased. Here, at the London Victoria, she fitted in. And life was going to be just fine.

The question papers were finally marked by the emergency department's team. 'And the winner—by a clear ten points—is the paediatric team,' Max Fenton announced. 'Well done. You get the tin of biscuits this month. But don't think you're going to make it two in a row, Morgan,' he informed the paediatrics consultant. 'We're still in the lead overall.'

'By all of two quizzes. Don't count your chickens.' Rhys laughed. 'We have a secret weapon now.'

'Who could just as well be on our team,' Max said, 'given that the PAU has such a crossover with the emergency department.'

'Hands off. She's ours,' Rhys said.

Stephanie was pretty sure that it was just friendly bickering, but even so she judged it politic to disappear to the toilet until any ruffled feathers had been smoothed over.

On the way back, she discovered that all the teams had merged and groups of people were sitting at different tables. Not quite sure which one to join, she paused and scanned the room.

'Hey, Stephanie.'

Relieved at not being totally deserted, she turned towards the voice.

Daniel Connor.

He smiled at her. 'Seeing as you wiped the floor with us, will you let me buy you a celebratory drink?'

Did he mean as a colleague?

If she could pigeonhole him just as a friend and colleague, and ignore the way her heart seemed to do a backflip every time he smiled, it would be fine. OK, so she knew he was single, which meant there was no reason why he shouldn't ask her to have a drink with him as more than just a friendly gesture from a colleague; but she was pretty sure that he had as much emotional baggage as she did. She had no idea how long ago he'd lost his wife, and she wouldn't dream of asking, but for all she knew he could still be healing. Just as she was. Neither of them needed any complications.

'Stephanie?' he prompted.

She had to answer now. 'A drink from a colleague would be lovely.' Just to make the terms clear. 'Thank you.'

'What would you like?'

'Sparkling water, please.'

'I'll just go and get our drinks. Have a seat.'

She noticed that he, too, was drinking mineral water when he returned with their glasses. Because he was on call, so he needed to keep a clear head in case of an emergency? Or because he was a single parent, and couldn't afford the luxury of a couple of glasses of wine, in case his daughter woke and needed him in the night?

Not that it was any of her business.

'So how come your general knowledge is so amazing?' Daniel asked.

She smiled. 'Misspent youth.' Which he could interpret how he liked. She wasn't going to tell him that it was from growing up with her nose in a book to keep the outside world at a safe distance. She'd read and read and read, and absorbed everything.

'I'm impressed. And I'm trying to work out how I can annex you for our team, next time round.'

This time, she laughed. 'Sorry. Max Fenton's already suggested that to Rhys and got short shrift.'

'I'm not Max.' He tapped his nose and grinned.

'I still don't rate your chances.' She turned her glass round in her hands. 'I meant to say, I'm sorry about your wife. It must be hard for you.'

'Yeah, it was very hard when she was killed.' He grimaced. 'I might as well tell you now and get the pity party out of the way.'

Oh, no. She hadn't been fishing. 'You really don't have to say anything,' she backtracked hastily. 'I'm sorry. I didn't mean to be nosey.'

'It's natural to wonder. And I'd rather you heard it from me than from anyone else.' He looked sad. 'It was a freak accident, four years ago. Mia was only two at the time. An elderly driver panicked when she was parking her car and she hit the accelerator instead of the brake. She ended up driving over the pavement and mowing Meg down. We were lucky that Mia wasn't killed, too—Meg had the presence of mind to shove the pushchair out of the way when she realised the car wasn't going to stop.'

Stephanie stared at him, shocked. 'I'm so sorry. What an awful thing to happen.'

'Not just for me. Meg's family lost their daughter, Mia lost her mum, my family lost Meg…and the old lady who killed her probably still has nightmares about it. She was in bits at the inquest—but it *was* an accident. It's not as if she meant to run Meg over like that.' He shrugged.

'Sometimes I wonder what would've happened if she'd given up driving when her family asked her to, instead of being stubborn and insisting that she could still do it and they were trying to take away her independence. Meg would probably still be alive. Mia might have a brother or sister. We'd probably have a dog.' He blew out a breath. 'But it's pointless torturing myself over it because nothing I can do will ever make a difference. And I have a lot of good things in life. I have Mia and my family and Meg's family.'

Yeah. He was definitely lucky there. Not that Stephanie intended to say that. It would be too crass.

'And they all chip in to help with Mia.' He smiled. 'Mum does the school run for me in the mornings if I'm on an early shift. My sister, Lucy, happens to be a teacher at Mia's school, so she'll take Mia home if I'm on a late, provided she doesn't have a meeting. If she's got a meeting, then Meg's mum picks Mia up and gives her dinner. I'm really lucky.'

'And so is Mia, having so many people who really care about her.'

'Absolutely.' He smiled at her. 'So what's your story?'

The question threw her. 'I…er…'

'Married, children?' he asked.

Once, and almost, she thought. 'No story.' At least, not one she wanted to tell: a failed marriage; a failed surrogate pregnancy; and a failure at being part of a family.

'In other words, back off and stop being nosey,' he said.

She winced. 'Sorry. I didn't mean to be that sharp. You weren't being nosey. I've noticed that everyone's very close here, at the London Victoria, and they look out for each other.'

'And at your last hospital it was a bit more private?'

It was a let-out, and she took it gratefully. 'Something like that. And there isn't a story. I'm just a boring divorcée.'

Oh, there was a story, all right. Daniel recognised the barriers Stephanie was busy putting up; he'd spent enough of the last four years doing something similar. Keeping people at a little more of a distance, except for his family, and evading all the attempts by well-meaning friends and his mother to fix him up with a date to help him move on from the past. And if he pushed Stephanie too hard right now, he had a feeling she'd do exactly what he'd done in the past and make an excuse to leave early. It took courage to join in with inter-departmental events when you had a past to live down.

'Message received and understood,' he said easily.

Stephanie looked relieved that she didn't have to explain any further, especially when Daniel steered the conversation back to more normal things—how long she'd been in the department, how she'd settled in and what the differences were between the London Victoria and her old hospital in Manchester.

'I do hope you're not trying to poach our new quiz star for the maternity team, Dan,' Rhys Morgan said, coming to stand by their table.

'If you are,' Katrina said, 'then I'll be having a word with my cousin.'

'Cousin?' Stephanie looked at her. 'You have family working in the maternity ward?'

'Maddie Petrakis,' Katrina confirmed. 'She's part time at the moment. You might have met Theo, her husband.'

'My boss,' Daniel said. 'Who's not here tonight, or you lot might've been buying us the celebratory drinks.'

'In your dreams, Dan—you know the last round's always between us and Max's lot,' Rhys said with a grin. 'Actually, I'm seeing Theo on Monday about a cross-departmental project. Stephanie, I want to talk to you about that, too.'

'And you can talk to her on *Monday*, Rhys,' Katrina cut in. 'You're both off duty right now.'

'I know. And we have a babysitter to relieve,' Rhys added. He kissed Katrina lingeringly. 'I get the message. I'll shut up. Let's go home. See you later, Stephanie.'

'See you on Monday,' Stephanie said with a smile, then turned to Daniel. 'You must have a babysitter to relieve, too.'

Well, of course she'd know that. She'd treated Mia. But

Daniel was intrigued by the difference between the bright, confident doctor in the PAU and this slightly diffident woman who'd drawn such huge barriers round herself. At the same time, it worried him that she intrigued him. OK, so it had been four years since Meg had died, but he wasn't ready to think about another relationship—not when he had Mia to put first—and he was pretty sure that Stephanie had emotional baggage, too. So it would be much more sensible to keep things to strictly colleagues.

Though he could still be kind to a new colleague.

'My parents are babysitting,' he confirmed. 'But I can give you a lift home, if you like.'

'No, you're fine, but thanks for the offer. See you later,' she said, and beat a hasty retreat. Just as he did, he thought wryly, when anyone tried to get too close to him.

Daniel filled Stephanie's thoughts as she walked home. If she was honest with herself then, yes, she did find him attractive. She'd already warmed to his personality, and his smile and cornflower-blue eyes could make her heart skip a beat. Now she knew for sure that he was single, there were no barriers to her acting on that attraction.

Apart from the fact that he came with complications. Daniel was a widower who'd lost his wife in incredibly tragic circumstances. OK, so it had been four years ago now, but that didn't mean he was in any way over what had happened, even though he was able to talk about it.

And he had a daughter. Mia seemed a very sweet child, but no doubt she missed having a mum; she was the odd one out at school. Stephanie could relate to that. Mia had lost her mum at the age of two, and Stephanie hadn't been much older than that herself when her own mum had died. Though Mia still had her dad. Stephanie had had only herself to rely on.

And, more to the point, Daniel had a close family. *Including in-laws.*

Her own in-laws had never really been able to accept her; Daniel's in-laws would no doubt find it hard to see him dating anyone else, feeling that she was trying to take their late daughter's place, so they'd have extra reasons not to accept her on top of the ones that Joe's family had had.

So it would be better to stick to being just colleagues. And she'd be sensible and keep a little bit of distance between herself and Daniel Connor in future.

CHAPTER THREE

'Dr Scott. Just the person I wanted to see.' Rhys smiled at Stephanie. 'I wanted a quick chat. Can you come into my office for a minute?'

'Sure.' This had to be the project Rhys had mentioned on Friday night after the quiz, she thought.

'So how are you settling in?' he asked, gesturing to her to take a seat.

'Fine. Everyone's been very welcoming. And I'm enjoying the work—it's really good that we can work with the emergency department staff in the paediatric assessment unit.'

'I'm glad. Actually, that's what I wanted to talk to you about. I'm working on another cross-departmental project to see how we can improve liaison between teams and give better patient care.'

'Which sounds perfectly sensible to me,' she said. 'Having the PAU in the emergency department works well.'

'And obviously we work closely with the maternity department.'

Where Daniel worked. Stephanie's pulse leapt. Stupid. She forced herself to concentrate. This was work, and Daniel was purely a colleague. 'Of course. We need to check the baby immediately after a complicated birth, and do the standard early postnatal checks, as well as following up any issues. Once the mum's been signed off, then the baby would come to us if there's a health problem.'

'Exactly. I'd like you to be part of the team working with the maternity department. Apart from anything else, it means you'll get to know a few more people a bit more quickly, too. Is that OK with you?' Rhys asked.

'That's fine,' she said with a smile. 'Thanks for the opportunity.'

'Good. I'll give Theo a call, and whoever's on his team can liaise with you.'

Stephanie was writing up her notes after a ward round when there was a knock on the open door of her office. She looked up to see Daniel.

Oh, help. Her stomach really wasn't supposed to be filled with butterflies like this. Even if he did have the most amazing blue eyes and a smile that made the room feel as if it had just been lit up. He was her colleague—*just* her colleague—and she'd already told herself that enough times to know better. She knew that relationships didn't work for her. How ridiculous was it to let herself react to him like this?

She took a deep breath and willed herself to calm down. 'Hello, Dr Connor.'

'Dan,' he corrected her. 'I can see you're busy, but can I have a quick word? Maybe later, if you're up to your eyes?'

'Now's fine. You know how it is with paperwork; it's always going to be there. What can I do for you?'

'I believe Rhys has talked to you about the team liaison project?'

'Yes.' Suddenly it all fell into place. 'Does that mean you're on the maternity team for the project?'

He nodded. 'So it looks as if this one is down to you and me. Are you busy at lunchtime?'

Which was her let-out. She opened her mouth to say yes, but the wrong words came out. 'If you call having a sandwich and going for a walk busy.'

'How about we have a sandwich and a walk together?' he suggested.

Oh, help. This was beginning to sound like a date. And she could feel the colour rising in her cheeks to betray her.

'We can talk about the project and work out what we need to do.' He wrinkled his nose. 'I know it's a bit of a cheek, asking you to give up your lunch break for work.'

Work. Of course it was just work. She seized the excuse gratefully. 'No, it's fine. Otherwise we're going to have to fit in a meeting between patients—and one of us is bound to be needed in the middle of it.'

'Or just before a shift starts or after it ends, and we might not be rostered on at the same time. I thought we'd both be more likely to be around at lunchtime,' Daniel said.

'Good idea. OK. I'll see you at lunchtime, then.'

'Great. I'll call for you.' He smiled and was gone, leaving her to her paperwork.

Odd how that smile made her feel warm inside.

Stupid, too. This was about work, and nothing but work. They were having lunch together simply because it was the easiest way to fit in a meeting. And her common sense had better come back, pronto.

For once, the ward was quiet, so Daniel was able to call for Stephanie as they'd agreed. They picked up a meal from the hospital canteen; he noticed that she chose a healthy chicken salad wrap, fruit and water. Clearly she was someone who looked after herself, rather than a lot of the medics he knew, who grabbed a chocolate bar for quick energy because they didn't have time for a proper break and a proper meal. Then they walked out to the park opposite the hospital and found a seat.

'So how was your morning?' she asked.

She really did have an amazing smile, he thought. Crazily, although they were outside and it was already sunny, the whole park felt brighter when she smiled. 'Fine. Yours?'

'Fine. Well, full of paperwork,' she said ruefully. 'And I guess this is going to be more of the same.'

Daniel found it hard to concentrate on talking to her about the roles of their departments and where they could work together to give their patients better care. He wanted to reach over and touch her dark hair, see if it was as soft as it looked. Which was insane; he never normally acted this way towards anyone.

But Stephanie looked so cute, all serious and thoughtful as she made notes on her mobile phone while they discussed the ins and outs of their respective departments.

For a mad moment, he itched to lean over and touch his mouth to hers. Just once. Just to see what it felt like.

'Dan?' she asked.

'Uh.' He felt the betraying heat crawling into his face. 'Sorry, I was multi-tasking. I should know better. I don't have enough X chromosomes to do that sort of thing.'

She laughed and the seriousness in her face vanished. She really *was* pretty, Daniel thought. He liked the way her green eyes crinkled at the corners, even at the same time as it scared him. He didn't notice things like this about women. He didn't think of women in terms of anything other than family, colleagues or patients. This woman could be seriously dangerous to his peace of mind.

'Don't do yourself down,' she said. 'Or do you normally hang around with totally sexist women?'

He laughed back. 'Would a bossy little sister count?'

Her smile faded then, and he wondered what he'd said to change her mood.

Not that he could ask. There were suddenly barriers a mile high round her, and she kept the rest of their conversation on a totally businesslike footing. By the time they'd finished their lunch, she had enough notes for the basis of a report. 'I'll type it up and email it over to you, so you can see if I've missed anything.'

'Thanks, that'd be good.'

And he couldn't get the easiness back between them when they walked back to the hospital. He had no idea what he'd said to upset her, but he'd definitely rattled her cage.

'Daddy, Ellie in my class is going to be a bridesmaid,' Mia said, when Daniel had finished reading her bedtime story that evening.

'That's nice, darling,' he said.

'She's going to have a really pretty dress. A purple one.'

Where was his daughter going with this? he wondered.

'I'd like to be a bridesmaid.' Her brown eyes were earnest.

Daniel relaxed and ruffled her hair. 'I'm sure you'd make a lovely bridesmaid. Maybe one day.'

'Maybe Aunty Lucy will get married,' Mia said.

Given that his sister was still recovering from the break-up of her first marriage, he wasn't sure that'd happen any time soon. Not that it was a topic he wanted to discuss with a six-year-old. 'Maybe.'

'Ellie's going to have a new mummy,' Mia added thoughtfully. 'Because her daddy's getting married. That's why she's going to be a bridesmaid.'

Oh, help. Now he could see where she was really going with this.

'And she's not like Snow White's nasty stepmother. She's really nice. She taught Ellie how to draw cats.' Mia bit her lip. 'Ellie's so lucky. She's going to have two mummies.'

And Mia didn't even have one.

Had he been selfish, avoiding everyone's attempts to fix him up on a date? Should he have put his own feelings aside and tried to find someone who'd fit into their lives and be a mother to Mia? Guilt seeped through him.

'Yes, she's lucky,' he said softly. 'But you're lucky, too. You have two nannas. And Aunty Lucy.'

'Ye-es.'

But he knew that having two grandmothers and an aunt weren't the same as having a mum. And now he felt really bad because he'd effectively stopped his daughter talking about her feelings. He could see that she was hurting.

'Your mummy loved you very much,' he said, stroking her hair. 'And so do I.'

'Love you, too, Daddy,' Mia said.

'Sleep tight, angel.' OK, so he was being selfish again, backing away from the conversation—but he didn't know what to say to her. How to make it right. Because this was something he couldn't fix. 'See you in the morning.'

'Night-night, Daddy.' Mia snuggled under her duvet after he'd kissed her goodnight.

Daniel thought about it for the rest of the evening.

He was still thinking about it, the next day. A mum for Mia.

Could he do this? Find her a mother? Replace Meg in his life as well as in hers?

After all, he had met someone. The first woman he'd been attracted to since Meg's death. Though that in itself made him feel horribly guilty, as if he were betraying Meg's memory. Mia had made it clear that she wanted a mother figure in her life; or was it just a phase? How would she feel if he started seeing someone? Would she feel as if she was missing out on time with him?

And then there was Stephanie herself. She'd been cagey about her past, and Daniel was pretty sure that someone had hurt her. Badly. Like him, she might have filled her life so she didn't have space for a relationship. And, even if she did have space, would she want to get involved with someone who already had a child?

He brooded about it all the way home.

His sister was curled up on the sofa, reading, when he walked in; she looked up and frowned. 'Tough day?' she asked.

'I'm fine,' he lied.

'Dan, I've known you long enough to see the signs. Come and sit down in the kitchen. I saved you some pasta. While it's heating through, you can talk.'

'Lucy, you're being bossy.' But he followed her into the kitchen and sat down at the table anyway.

'I'm worried about you, Dan.' She put the pasta in the microwave and sat down opposite him. 'Tell me.'

'I don't know where to start.' He sighed. 'Mia was saying yesterday that one of her friends is getting a second mum.'

'That would be Ellie.' Lucy nodded. 'Her new step-mum's very nice.'

'Mia, um, kind of hinted that she wants a mum.'

'And that's upset you?'

'Thrown me.' He grimaced. 'Lucy, do you think it would be wrong of me to see someone?'

'That depends. If you're doing it just to give Mia a mum, then yes. That wouldn't be fair to any of you.' She paused. 'But if you've met someone *you* want to see, that's different. Mum and I have been saying for ages that you could do with some fun in your life. We all love Mia dearly, but it's hard being a single parent, and the only things you ever do are if you go out somewhere with us or if it's a team night at work.'

'Which makes it sound as if I don't have a social life.'

'You *don't* have a social life,' she said gently.

He rubbed his jaw. 'I feel guilty. It's—well, it feels as if I'm betraying Meg.'

'Rubbish,' Lucy said roundly. 'Think of it the other way round—if you'd been the one killed in the accident, would you have wanted Meg to be on her own for the rest of her life?'

'I'm not on my own,' he said. 'I have Mia, I have you, I have Mum and Dad, and I have the Parkers.'

'Having a daughter and a supportive family who love you,' Lucy pointed out, 'isn't the same as dating someone. You're still young, Dan. You're only thirty-five, but you're acting as if you're an old man.'

He had no answer to that.

'Would you have wanted Meg to stay on her own?'

He sighed. 'No. I would've wanted her to find someone who'd love her as much as I did. Someone who'd treat Mia as his own and love her, too.'

'Exactly. And Meg was my friend as well as my sister-in-law. I knew her well enough to know how she would've felt—and she would've felt the same as you do.' She paused. 'So have you met someone?'

He didn't answer. Not that it made any difference.

'Why don't you ask her out?' Lucy asked.

He gave her a speaking look. Wasn't it obvious?

Lucy spread her hands. 'What's the worst that could happen?' When he didn't answer, she said it for him. 'That she says no. And then it's no different from the situation you're in now, not going out with her. Ask her.'

He wrinkled his nose. 'It might be a bit awkward at work.'

'She works with you?'

'Sort of,' he hedged.

'In the same department?'

He had to be honest. 'No.'

'Well, then. It won't be awkward. You always put patients first and you're professional. OK, it might be a *little* bit awkward at the first team night out afterwards, but it'll soon smooth over.' She leaned over and squeezed his hand. 'You're scared, aren't you?'

Trust his sister to work that out. 'It's been a long time since I've dated. I have no idea what I'm doing.' He dragged in a breath. 'And it's not fair to Mia. Or to this woman.'

'Whoa, you're really building bridges to trouble here. Look, there's a world of difference between going out with someone and enjoying an evening in each other's company, and asking the woman to marry you and become Mia's stepmother.'

'I guess.'

'Mia doesn't have to know anything about this, so she's not going to get hurt. If it doesn't work out between you and the mystery woman, then it doesn't work out, but you've still had a couple of nice evenings out and had some fun, for a change. And if it does work out—well, you've already said Mia wants a mum.'

How easy she made it sound. 'You make it sound so easy,' he said lightly.

She laughed. 'It sounds easy, but we both know it isn't always. Don't forget I made a pretty good mess of my own love life. Dan, you don't have to be perfect. You just have to be yourself.'

'Harvey was an idiot, you know.' He'd never liked her ex.

'And so was I, for choosing him, but I've forgiven myself for that.'

Daniel felt his eyes widen as he absorbed her words. 'Lucy, are *you* seeing someone?'

'I might be.'

He folded his arms and waited.

She gave in and groaned. 'If you tell Mum, you're toast. I don't want her getting her hopes up, not until I know where this is going.'

He laughed. 'OK, this is just between you and me. What's he like and where did you meet him? Did Karen finally talk you into doing that online dating thing?'

'No, he's a parent at the school—not the parent of anyone I teach,' she added swiftly. 'I met him at a school governor meeting.'

So the man had a social conscience and was happy to do his bit for the community—unlike Harvey, who was the most selfish man Daniel had ever met. That was a good start. 'You deserve someone nice—and you can tell him that your big brother—'

'I'm telling him nothing of the kind,' she cut in, 'and, much as I love you, Dan, I don't need you to fight my corner every second of the day. Just as you don't need me there every second, fighting your corner.' She softened her words with a smile. 'But I'm glad we talked about this. Mum worries about you, and so do I. You need to do something for *you*, Dan. You're more than just Mia's dad and a busy doctor.'

He didn't quite see how he could fit anything else into his life. But he smiled at his sister, knowing that she meant well. 'The same goes for you. You're more than just a brilliant teacher and aunt.'

She laughed. 'I know. And I'm doing something about it. So maybe it's time for you to do something about it, too. Ask her out, Dan. You'll never know what she'd say unless you do.'

He thought about it for the next couple of days, and decided that maybe his sister was right. The next time he saw Stephanie, he'd ask her out.

But their shifts were clearly out of sync, because she didn't attend any of the births where there were enough complications for the midwives to involve him and need a paediatrician on standby.

He made the decision when she emailed him the report. He emailed back.

Can we have a quick discussion? When's good for you?

The reply came.

Lunch today or tomorrow, patients permitting?

Sure. I'll ring down and see if you're free.

He spent the rest of the morning doing the ward rounds, reassuring the nervous first-time mums and double-checking the obs for one of his mums with suspected pre-eclampsia before asking the midwives to step up the frequency and call him the minute anything changed. And then he called Stephanie's extension.

'Paediatrics, Stephanie Scott speaking,' she said.

'It's Dan. Are OK for a lunch meeting about the project today?' he asked.

'Yes. I'll meet you at the canteen. I think we'll have to give the park a miss today.'

He glanced out of the window and realised that it was absolutely bucketing down outside. It looked more like November than September outside. Definitely not the right weather for lunch outdoors. 'OK. See you there.'

Funny how his heart skipped a beat when he walked down the corridor and saw Stephanie waiting for him at the door to the canteen.

He kept himself in check and steered the conversation over lunch to her report and his suggested amendments, agreeing them with her point by point. And then, at the end, he looked at her. 'Stephanie, before you rush back to the department, are you free any evening this week?'

She looked started. 'Free?'

Oh, help. How was he going to ask her without it sounding sleazy or needy? It had been ten years since he'd last asked someone out. He was way out of practice in the dating game. Then he remembered what Lucy had said. Just be himself. The worst that could happen was that she'd say no.

'I, um, thought might be nice to have dinner together. If you're not busy,' he added swiftly.

And he didn't dare look at her. In case he saw disgust— or, worse, pity.

Would she say yes?

Or would she make a polite excuse and then be cool with him from here on after?

CHAPTER FOUR

STEPHANIE COULDN'T QUITE believe this. She hadn't dated since she'd been a student—since she'd met Joe—and it really wasn't something she was good at. She'd married the last man—ha, the *first* man—she'd dated; and that had turned out to be a complete disaster.

She shook herself. Daniel was asking her out to dinner, not shoving an engagement ring at her and asking her to spend the rest of her life with him. But, even so, panic flooded through her. 'If this is about me looking after Mia when she was ill, there's really no need—I was just doing my job, the same as you do with your mums and babies.'

'It's not about Mia. It's about you and me, and—' He stopped. 'Sorry, I'm hopeless at this. I haven't asked anyone out for a long time.'

Was she the first person he'd asked out since his wife had died? Oh, help. That was extra pressure she didn't need. How could she be mean enough to knock him back, under those circumstances? Then again, how could she be mean enough to say yes, knowing that she was an emotional mess and totally hopeless when it came to relationships?

'I really should've gone on one of those online dating site things and brushed up on how you ask someone out,' Daniel said wryly.

His candour made her feel a lot better and she smiled at him. He was obviously feeling as out of his depth as she was, right now; and he obviously wasn't taking anything for granted. 'That makes two of us. I mean, not that I ask people out. I just haven't dated for a while and—oh, dear.' She grimaced. 'I think I'm digging a hole for both of us.'

He smiled back at her. 'I think we need to start this one again. My sister said I should just be myself and be honest.'

He'd talked to his sister about her?

Stephanie went cold. Clearly Daniel was close to his sister; he'd already told Stephanie that she babysat for him and sometimes picked his daughter up from school. But Stephanie had been there before with a man who was close to his sister. It had ended in tears—and not just hers.

Then again, there was no reason to assume that Daniel's sister would be anything like Joe's sister. Besides, why was she assuming that he'd even introduce her to his sister? She really was putting the cart before the horse here, and she needed to stop this right now. What was her best friend always telling her about never troubling trouble until trouble troubles you? She dragged in a breath to help damp down the panic, but she still didn't have a clue what to say.

Daniel didn't seem to let her silence throw him, though. 'Stephanie, I like you and I'd like to get to know you better outside work. Would you have dinner with me one evening?'

That was as clear as it could get. Almost. She knew that Daniel came as a package, so there was just one tiny thing to clarify. 'Just you and me?' she checked.

He nodded. 'Look, you know I'm a single dad. It wouldn't be fair to Mia to introduce her to anyone I date until we know exactly where the relationship is going and we're both sure it's the right thing to do. So for now this is just you and me, and—um—we'll just see how it goes?'

No expectations. No pressure. Just getting to know each other. That worked for her. 'OK. I'd like that. Thank you. Well, I'm on an early shift on—' She grabbed her phone and checked the calendar function. 'Wednesday and Thursday.'

He checked his own calendar. 'Sorry, I'm on a late. How about next week?'

'My early shifts are Monday and Tuesday,' she said.

He nodded. 'I can do Tuesday.'

'Great. We can sort out when and where—well, some time before Tuesday.' She bit her lip, knowing that she was being a total coward but unable to stop herself. 'I'd better get back to the ward.'

'Me, too,' he said. 'And I'll look forward to Tuesday next week.'

Stephanie found that her concentration was shot to pieces for the rest of the day. It was fine when she was with a patient—she could focus on keeping her patient calm, doing any tests and carrying out any treatment needed, and explaining any treatment to the patient's parents. But once it came to sorting out the paperwork, she found herself wool-gathering. Thinking about Daniel. Wondering if they were doing the right thing. Wondering if it was twenty years too soon for her to date again.

She needed to talk to someone about this.

And there was only one person she trusted enough to talk to. So when she got home after her shift, she called her best friend.

'Hey, Steffie. How are you?' Trish said, sounding pleased to hear from her.

'Fine,' Stephanie fibbed. 'Trish…are you busy? I mean, I know you are, but is now a good time to talk?'

'Harry's asleep and I'm just flicking through the chan-

nels while Jake's at the gym. So now's absolutely fine.'
Trish paused. 'What's wrong, sweetie?'

'Nothing's *wrong* exactly. Just...' She blew out a breath,
not sure what to say.

'I really wish you were still just round the corner instead of a couple of hundred miles away. I'd tell you to
come straight over with a bottle of wine and we'd talk.'

Which was exactly why Stephanie was calling her. Because right now she really needed to talk. Get the confu-
sion in her head straightened out. 'I've, um, been asked
out to dinner.'

'And you don't want to go?'

'I do—but it's complicated. He's a widower.'

'Much older than you?'

'Three or four years, maybe. He has a six-year-old
daughter.'

Trish was silent.

'You think this is a bad idea, don't you?' Stephanie
asked.

'I think,' Trish said carefully, 'a date could be good
for you.'

'But?' Even though her best friend hadn't actually said
the word, Stephanie knew she was thinking it.

Trish sighed. 'Steffie, it sounds like everything you've
always wanted. A ready-made family. And, yes, that does
worry me.'

Stephanie knew exactly why Trish was worrying. Because of Joe. Because of the way her marriage had imploded. Because of the baby she hadn't been able to carry
to term for Joe's sister. On paper, this was the promise of
having everything she'd lost: a partner and a child. A family. Like she'd never, ever had.

She bit her lip. 'It isn't quite like that. Mia doesn't know
about me. Well, obviously she knows I exist, because I

treated her at the hospital—that's how I met Daniel—but he isn't telling her that we're dating. Right now we're taking it slowly and seeing what happens.'

'If you were sitting here right now on the sofa with me, you'd see the relief in my face,' Trish said.

'So you *do* think it's a bad idea.'

'Dating someone? No. All I'm saying is don't rush into it. Have some fun.' Trish paused. 'But don't build your hopes up. Don't take it too seriously. Don't put the cart before the horse.'

'Or trouble trouble. I know. It's not going to be another Joe situation,' Stephanie said.

Trish blew out a breath. 'That wasn't your fault, Steffie, and you know it.'

Stephanie loved her friend for her loyalty, but she also knew it wasn't a completely fair comment. 'I have to take my share of the blame for it going wrong. I'm not very good at families.'

'You're good with mine,' Trish pointed out.

'Mmm. But that's different. Your family's *nice*.' And they'd accepted her for who she was; Joe's family had been judgemental right from the start, never quite accepting her as one of them.

Trish laughed. 'You have a point. So when are you going out on this date?'

'Next Tuesday night.'

'Doing?'

'I don't actually know, yet. Dinner, probably.'

'Good. Have fun. And call me when you get back so you can tell me how it went.'

The phone was the next best thing to going over to Trish's house and talking about it, but it wasn't the same. Stephanie realised again just how much she missed her best friend. 'I will,' she promised. 'Anyway, enough about me. How are you, and how's my godson?'

Just as she'd hoped, Trish was happy to chatter about her son and how he was doing at nursery. And it helped to distract Stephanie from the worries about whether she really was doing the right thing.

Dinner. Was that too intimate for a first date, Daniel wondered, especially given that Stephanie had admitted to being divorced, which meant she probably had scars? Should he have suggested something else?

Which was all fine, but he had no idea what. He was well out of practice when it came to dating.

He waited until Mia was in bed, then looked online to see if he could find any suggestions about first-time dates. His first attempt netted him an article with ten suggestions, and he skimmed down them. The problem was, he didn't know her well enough to know her tastes, and he certainly wasn't going to ask around at work. He didn't want any speculation.

He was about to give up when he saw the last suggestion. Play the tourist. Actually, that might be a nice idea, because he knew she'd moved here from Manchester and didn't know the city that well.

This time, he typed in 'London attractions'. Museums, the London Eye, the Tower of London… And then he saw a link to an exhibition that sounded intriguing. When he clicked onto the site to read more, he loved the sound of it: a room where you could walk through it with rain falling down, but you didn't get wet because the rain was controlled by a computer that could sense your movement and stopped the rain from falling on you.

He texted Stephanie before he lost his nerve.

Tuesday, fancy doing something mad before dinner?

The reply came back sooner than he'd hoped.

Such as?

He typed in the link to the website of the exhibition.
If she hated the idea, he had plenty of time to look for
something else.

There was a long pause and he thought he'd blown it.
He should've suggested something more sensible. Now
she was going to think he was totally flaky; he was out of
his depth, who was going to want to date a single dad and
face all the complications that went with that?

When his phone eventually beeped, he felt sick as he
opened the text message. He had to read it three times to
make sure it really said what he thought it said.

Sounds great. How fantastic that you found it :)

Relief flooded through him. This might just work out.

Meet you there at seven?

Mia would be in bed by then, so he wouldn't miss out
on any time with her; plus the queue for the art installation would probably have died down by then.

Seven's fine. Thank you :)

It felt like months until Tuesday finally arrived. But Daniel
was standing outside the exhibition hall at three minutes
to seven. He had a feeling that Stephanie wasn't the type
to be 'fashionably' late, and he was relieved to discover
that he was right.

'You look nice,' he said. She was wearing flat shoes and a pale turquoise dress that made her dark hair look almost black.

She laughed. 'It's rainproof.'

'Rainproof?' The material didn't look remotely shiny or waterproof; it looked like soft, soft jersey. As soft as her skin might be.

'Well, not rainproof *exactly*. But I found a couple of articles about the installation online. They said if you wear dark clothes, you're more likely to get wet.'

He glanced at his own dark trousers and dark-coloured casual shirt and gave her a rueful smile. 'You could've told me that.'

She grinned. 'They might not be right. Given the colour of my hair, I hope they're not!'

He laughed. 'Let's go and find out.'

The queue wasn't too long, so they were soon in the exhibition. They walked very gingerly through the room.

'This is amazing. I can feel the moisture in the air and hear the rain falling, but you're right, we're not actually getting wet.'

'I did wonder if we ought to bring an umbrella, just in case,' he admitted.

She laughed. 'I'm glad you didn't. I love this. Doesn't it make you want to do that Gene Kelly routine?'

So she liked musicals. Maybe they could go to one together. He started humming 'Singing in the Rain', then gave her a sidelong look. 'Dare you.'

She wrinkled her nose. 'I'm not quite brave enough.'

'Neither am I,' Daniel said, though he knew he probably would've done it with Mia. Then again, he could get away with behaving playfully when he was with his daughter.

'This is amazing,' Stephanie said. 'I'm not normally

one for modern art, but this is really clever. Thank you so much for suggesting this.'

'My pleasure.' Daniel found himself relaxing again. 'Look, there's a couple over there dancing.'

'And a bunch of students obviously trying to find out how fast you have to move before the computer gets confused and lets you get wet,' she said, pointing them out.

They found themselves chatting easily as they walked through the installation—and neither of them got in the slightest bit wet.

Afterwards, they went to a nearby pizza place for dinner. Daniel discovered that they both loved Italian and Thai food, and Stephanie was a keen cook.

'My stuff tends to be simple,' he said. 'Mia's pretty good at trying new things, but she's at the age where she still prefers plain food to fancy stuff.'

'Nothing wrong with that,' Stephanie said with a smile. 'And she makes great cakes.'

'Yeah.' Daniel had to swallow the lump in his throat.

At the end of the evening, he said, 'I'll see you home.'

'Thanks, but there's no need. I know Manchester's not as big as London, but it's still a city, so I'm used to looking after myself in a city.'

'Sorry. I didn't mean to be patronising. Just I was brought up—'

'—to be a gentleman,' she finished. 'Which is sweet. But I'm fine.'

So now they'd go their separate ways. What now? Did he kiss her goodnight? Or would that be too much pressure? It had been so long since he'd dated, he'd forgotten all the rules. 'Well—I guess I'll see you at work.'

'Yup.'

Would she take that as a brush-off? He could ask her out again; or would that be too pushy? He decided to take the risk. 'I, um, enjoyed this evening. Maybe we could do something like this again?'

She smiled. 'I enjoyed it, too. And, yes, I'd like to go out again.'

Her reaction gave him courage. 'Let's synchronise our off duty,' he said.

'OK. I'll text you my schedule when I get home.'

'That'd be good.' He wondered if kissing her cheek would be OK. But then he realised that he'd dithered too long. Doing it now would be awkward. 'I'll talk to you later, then. Goodnight.'

'Goodnight, Dan. And thanks for this evening.'

CHAPTER FIVE

WHEN STEPHANIE WENT onto the maternity ward, the next day, Daniel was there; he smiled at her and she could feel herself blushing. 'Hi, there. I've come to do the rounds and the newborn checks.'

He walked with her to the midwives' desk. 'We have three newborns for you this morning—it was a busy day, yesterday.'

Iris, the senior midwife, said, 'I'm a little worried about one of the new mums, Janine. She's not bonding with her baby at all and she's showing no interest in him, even when we encourage her.'

'Postnatal depression?' Stephanie asked.

'I think she's a bit shell-shocked, the poor love.' Iris grimaced. 'The poor kid's only just turned sixteen.'

The same age as Stephanie's mother had been at Stephanie's birth. Stephanie felt a flood of sympathy. 'Do you want me to see if I can get her to talk to me when I check the baby?'

'If you can, that'd be good,' Iris said. 'Thanks, Stephanie.'

'I'll come with you and introduce you to the first of our mums,' Daniel said.

'Thanks.' Stephanie returned his smile and thought again how easy it was to work with him.

She left Janine until last so she'd time to spend with the girl; it wouldn't matter if the consultation ran over into her break. She introduced herself to Janine. 'Hello, I'm Dr Stephanie Scott, and I'm here to do the newborn check on your baby.' A quick glance showed her that the girl didn't have any congratulations cards or flowers; she seemed totally alone. 'Is that OK, or would you like someone to be here with you while I'm checking your baby?'

The girl simply shrugged and looked away.

Was she shy? Was she shocked by what was happening to her? Or did it go deeper than that? 'OK. Well, I'll talk you through what I'm doing and why.' She looked at baby, and noticed that the blue label on his cot said Baby Rivers; clearly Janine hadn't decided on a name yet. 'He's a beautiful boy,' she said. 'What are you going to call him?'

Another shrug. 'Don't know.'

Was this what it had been like for her own mother, Stephanie wondered, feeling that everyone who walked into the room would judge her and find her wanting? Thirty-two years ago, it would've been even tougher; not just the fact she wasn't married to the baby's father, but her age at the birth as well. Society had learned to be more accepting, but Stephanie knew that Janine was still going to face a tough time.

'It's hard to choose,' she said lightly. 'I'm going to start by looking at the baby's head.' She unwrapped him from the swaddling. 'It looks as if you needed a little bit of help to deliver him.'

Janine simply shrugged again.

'The forceps have left a little bit of a bruise on him, but it's nothing to worry about because it will clear up in a couple of days.' She checked the baby's fontanelles. 'His head looks absolutely fine to me. I'm going to check his eyes now—that means shining a light in his eyes to look for the reflex I expect to see, but it won't hurt him.'

Janine remained silent.

Stephanie performed the procedure. 'I'm glad to say that's fine, too, and there's no sign of cataracts. I'm going to check his mouth now. Are you feeding him yourself?'

Janine shook her head.

Stephanie smiled at her. 'Don't worry, I'm not going to pressure you to try to breastfeed him, though if you do want to try then any of the midwives would be happy to sit down with you and help you with the technique. It can be tricky at first.'

'I'm probably not going to keep him, so there's no point trying.'

But there was a wobble in the girl's voice. Did that mean she wanted to keep the baby and someone was pressuring her to give him up? Again, Stephanie thought of her own mother, the coldness of her parents and the pressure she'd been under.

She sat on the bed. 'Janine, I know you're very young and it's an awful lot to take in, but if you want to keep your baby then we can help you.'

Janine looked away. 'They won't let me.'

They? Stephanie assumed the girl meant her parents. She could understand them being shocked that their daughter was pregnant so young, and underage, but at the same time surely they had to realise that their daughter really needed their support?

'We have people here who can talk to your mum and dad and reassure them that you'll get the support you need,' she said gently.

There was a glitter of tears in Janine's eyes. 'It's not my mum. If it was just her, we'd probably sort it out between us. It's *him*.'

'Your dad?'

Janine's chin came up and she looked stubborn and hurt. '*Not* my dad. Her husband.'

Now Stephanie began to understand. Janine's stepfather. There had probably already been tension between them before Janine had become pregnant. But, whatever his personal feelings, he was the adult and she was still a child. And it saddened Stephanie that someone would put so much pressure on a young, vulnerable girl at such a difficult time.

Cuddling the baby with one arm, she reached out to squeeze Janine's hand with her free hand. 'I know people who've been in your situation,' she said softly. 'And what you want is important, too. We can support you in the hospital. I can talk to the social services team if you want me to.'

Janine shook her head. 'He says he doesn't want do-gooders round our house, poking their nose in where it's not wanted.'

Poor kid, Stephanie thought. Her stepfather clearly had strong views, and no doubt had given the girl a hard time about falling pregnant. Even though it took two to make a baby.

She put her finger in the baby's mouth to check that there were no gaps in the roof of his mouth and his sucking reflex was working. When he sucked hard on her finger, she smiled. 'I think he's getting hungry.' She checked in his mouth to make sure that his tongue wasn't more anchored than it should be. 'Good, there are no signs of tongue-tie.'

She took her stethoscope out to listen to his breathing. 'Excellent—there's equal air entry into both lungs.' Then she listened to his heart. 'That's fine, too; there's no sign of a heart murmur or an irregular beat.'

Janine didn't reply.

Stephanie remembered the first time she'd heard her unborn baby's heartbeat. It had been magical and had made her want to bond with the baby, even though in the circumstances she knew she couldn't do that and had to stay detached. In the end, it had made no difference, and she'd wept for the baby when she'd lost it as much as any mother would've done.

Maybe this would help Janine, give her the strength to fight for the baby she clearly wanted and was too scared to keep.

'Do you want to listen?' she asked.

For a moment, she thought the girl would refuse. Then Janine's face brightened. 'Can I?'

'Sure you can.' She put the stethoscope on the girl's ears, then the other end over the baby's heart so Janine could hear it beating.

The girl smiled, and Stephanie was relieved to see that she was finally seeming interested in the baby.

Then a man walked into the room and stopped short as he saw them. 'What the hell are you doing?'

Hello to you, too, Stephanie thought, but put her most professional face on.

'I'm Dr Scott and I'm doing the newborn checks on Janine's baby.'

'Not you, I mean *her*.' He looked at Janine in disgust. 'There's no point in getting attached to the baby. You know full well we're not going to let you keep him.'

Janine looked cowed and shrank back into the bed.

So this must be the stepfather. No wonder the poor kid disliked him, Stephanie thought. He was a real martinet. He looked like an army sergeant major, with a very pristine appearance and shiny shoes and cropped hair. But Janine wasn't a soldier he could bark orders at. She was a vulnerable young girl who'd just given birth and needed a bit of sensitivity.

Stephanie wrapped the baby carefully to keep him warm, and put him back safely in the crib. She could finish the newborn checks in a minute. 'I'm afraid I'm going to have to ask you to leave.'

The man turned to her, his stance aggressive. 'Ask me to leave? Who the hell do you think you are?'

'I'm a paediatrician. And your behaviour is upsetting Janine and the baby.'

He bridled. 'That's none of your business.'

She kept her voice neutral. Just. 'Actually, it is my business while they're under my care.'

His lip curled, and she could tell that he was about to unleash a stream of venom at her. His mistake. She could more than look after herself; but this wasn't the place. A maternity unit was meant to be calm, not a battleground.

'I should perhaps remind you,' she said quietly, 'that we have a zero tolerance policy here at the London Victoria. Any abusive or intimidating behaviour towards staff or a patient is unacceptable. So you have two choices. You can leave now, or I can call Security.'

He leaned towards her, staring her down.

She stood her ground, refusing to let him intimidate her the way he'd cowed his stepdaughter. 'So you're happy for me to call Security to escort you out, then?'

A woman walked in, and looked wide-eyed as she saw the man's aggressive stance and Stephanie standing up to him. 'Bernie? What's going on?'

'This woman—' his voice was full of all the scorn he could muster '—is trying to throw me out.'

'We have a zero tolerance policy at the hospital,' Stephanie repeated.

Daniel came into the room. Clearly he'd overheard the

last bit, because he added, 'Which means anyone who abuses or intimidates staff or patients will be asked to leave, and if they won't leave we'll call Security and have them removed.'

'What the hell is it to do with you?' the man snarled.

'I'm the consultant on this ward.' Daniel's voice was very cool, very calm and very authoritative. 'I could hear you shouting across the other side of the ward. And I don't appreciate my mums or my colleagues being bullied. So it's your choice. You can lose the attitude, or you can leave the ward.'

Bernie curled his lip and grabbed the woman's hand. 'Come on, Gail. We're going.'

The woman looked at Janine and the baby, clearly torn between following her husband and wanting to see her daughter.

'Mum,' Janine whispered with an anguished expression, tears trickling down her face. *'Mum.'*

'Come on, Gail,' Bernie repeated, and jerked her hand to make her follow him.

They left, and Janine scrubbed at her eyes with the back of her hand.

'Are you OK, Janine?' Stephanie asked gently.

Janine bit her lip and said nothing. Clearly she was worried that there would be repercussions from what had just happened and her stepfather would give her an even harder time, the next time he saw her.

'OK. I'm going to finish checking over the baby now,' Stephanie said softly, and did so. 'Can you tell me if he's had a wet and dirty nappy since he was born?'

'Both,' Janine whispered.

'Thank you.' Stephanie continued with her checks, leaving the Moro reflex until last; the baby flung out both arms, spreading his fingers and stretching his legs, and started to cry.

Janine looked panicky. 'Is he all right?'

'Absolutely,' Stephanie reassured her. 'I've just checked his reflexes and the way he flung his arms out like that and cried shows that all's well.' She wrapped the baby up warm again and sat on the bed. 'I've pretty much finished checking him over now. He's a beautiful little boy, and you can be very proud of him.' She squeezed Janine's hand. 'Is there anyone I can call for you?'

'No. Thanks,' the girl added belatedly. 'I'll be all right.'

'OK. But the midwives are here to help. So are the doctors. If you want to talk to any of them, they'll listen. They've met plenty of people in your situation, so they know how to help.'

Janine nodded, but didn't look convinced.

'Take care,' Stephanie said, feeling helpless, and left the room.

Before she left the department, she caught up with Iris and Daniel. 'Three perfectly healthy babies, and nothing worrying to report, you'll be pleased to know.'

'Good,' Daniel said. 'We'll look forward to the paperwork.'

'About Janine,' she said. 'Her stepfather's clearly putting pressure on her to give the baby up. That's why she dare not let herself bond with the baby.'

Daniel grimaced. 'We can't interfere, Stephanie.'

'I know, but I'm not going to stand by and let him bully her. Yes, the baby wasn't planned, but it doesn't give him the right to treat her like that.'

'Be careful,' he said. 'You know we have to keep a professional distance from our patients.'

Oh, for pity's sake. Where was his compassion? Sometimes you had to do what your heart told you was the right thing. Clearly Daniel was as much of a stickler for the rules as Joe had been.

Which in turn meant that getting involved with him would be a bad idea. She'd already had one partner who'd wanted total control over her life. It wasn't a mistake she'd make again. Even though she'd enjoyed her date with Daniel, it was time to back off. 'I'll be in touch with the paperwork,' she said coolly, and left the department.

CHAPTER SIX

THE NEXT DAY, before her shift, Stephanie called in to see Janine with flowers and a card and a soft toy for the baby. Janine stared at them in seeming disbelief and a tear slid down her cheek.

'I didn't mean to upset you,' Stephanie said.

Janine gulped. 'You're the only one who's brought me a card and flowers. Even my best friend hasn't come to see me. We fell out, a few weeks ago, and she…' She bit her lip.

'Does she know you've had the baby?' Stephanie asked gently.

Janine shook her head.

'Call her and tell her,' Stephanie said. 'She'd want to know. It doesn't matter that you fell out.'

'And Mum didn't bring anything for the baby. Her first grandchild, and she doesn't want to know.' The tears really started to flow, and Stephanie sat on the edge of the bed and put her arms round the girl.

Once the tears had stopped, Janine said brokenly, 'My mum thinks I had a one-night stand and I don't know who the baby's dad is.' She dragged in a breath. 'It's not true. I'm not like that. She thinks I'm a cheap little tramp and a disappointment, the same as *he* thinks, but I'm not.'

'Of course you're not,' Stephanie soothed.

Janine cried into her shoulder again. 'He won't let me keep the baby.'

Stephanie knew the question she was about to ask was a difficult one, but if her suspicions were correct she couldn't possibly let Janine and the baby go back to that situation. 'Has your stepfather hit you?' Stephanie asked gently.

Janine shuddered. 'No. I thought he was going to when he found out about the baby, but Mum stopped him. He just shouted a lot and called me all kinds of names.'

'What about the baby's father?' Maybe he'd be able to support Janine.

She shook her head, looking terrified.

'You know who he is?' Stephanie checked.

Janine nodded and looked miserable.

'But he doesn't want to know?'

'He—' Janine choked '—he says there's no proof the baby's his.'

'A paternity test would prove it,' Stephanie pointed out quietly. 'And then he'd have to give you some support.' Financially, if not emotionally.

Janine shook her head. 'I don't want my baby anywhere near him.'

Stephanie frowned. 'Why not?'

'Because he—he—' Janine collapsed in tears again.

Stephanie rocked her until the weeping stopped. And then Janine whispered, 'He *made* me.'

Oh, the poor child. Stephanie's heart bled for her. 'Why didn't you tell your mum?' she asked gently.

Janine swallowed hard. 'I wasn't supposed to be at the party. Bernie had grounded me and I sneaked out to go.'

'OK, she probably would've been angry with you for that,' Stephanie said, 'but if you'd told her what happened she would've helped.'

Janine bit her lip. 'Ryan said nobody would believe me

if I told anyone. Everyone at school knew I fancied him, and he said he'd tell everyone I threw myself at him. I felt so dirty, so unclean.'

Stephanie really felt for the girl; she was so alone and had nowhere to turn. She couldn't help wondering, had it been like that for her own mother? 'Couldn't you have told a friend what happened? A teacher?'

Janine shook her head. 'And then my period was late. I knew what that meant but I didn't dare tell anyone. I kept hoping I'd wake up and it'd all be all right, but it just went on and on and I knew I was pregnant. I didn't need to do the test to know. I fainted at school and the school nurse worked it out.' She dragged in a breath. 'Mum was so angry with me. Bernie was even angrier. He said I'd let them both down and dragged their good name through the mud. I knew they wouldn't believe me if I told them about Ryan.'

'You need to tell them the truth,' Stephanie said gently. 'Then they'll understand and start supporting you.'

'What if they don't? What if they throw me out?' Janine looked panicky. 'I'm meant to go home tomorrow. If they throw me out I've got nowhere to go.'

That's exactly what happened to my mum, Stephanie thought. She couldn't lie to Janine and say that it definitely wouldn't happen—but there was one thing that had changed since her mother's pregnancy. 'I hope that won't happen, but if the worst *does* happen then you'll get proper support from social services. And I promise you I'll help with that.' She paused. 'What if I talk to your parents for you and tell them what really happened? If they shout at me, it won't matter.'

Janine shivered. 'You were going to have Bernie thrown out. He won't listen to you—he'll still be angry with you about that.'

'I'll make them listen,' Stephanie said.

'They still won't let me keep the baby,' Janine said.

'Is that what you want?'

The girl nodded. 'I know it's stupid, but my baby's the only one who'll love me for who I am. Ryan didn't love me; he was just using me for sex—and it was horrible.' She dragged in a breath. 'My mum doesn't really love me any more, now she's got Bernie. And he doesn't love me because I'm not the quiet, well-behaved girl he wants, the sort who only speaks when she's spoken to. He hates me because I've dyed my hair different colours and gone to parties. My skirts are too short and my heels are too high. I break all his rules and he just *hates* me for it.'

Stephanie thought again, Is this what my mum went through? 'I'll talk to them,' she promised.

Almost on cue, Janine's parents walked in. They stopped dead as they saw Janine crying.

'*You* again,' Bernie said with a curl to his lip.

'Yes, me,' Stephanie said calmly. She squeezed Janine's hand, and mouthed, *'Don't worry, everything's going to be fine.'* She turned back to her parents. 'I'm glad you're here. I was wondering if we could have a word.'

'Is something wrong with the baby?' Janine's mother said, looking worried.

'Perhaps if we could talk in a private room?' Stephanie said.

For a moment she thought that Janine's stepfather was going to refuse, but then he nodded. 'All right.'

She was relieved to spot Iris on their way out of Janine's room, and went over to her. 'I know it's a bit of a cheek, but can I borrow a room for a moment?'

'Sure.' She glanced at Janine's parents and back at her. 'Do you want me to get Daniel as back-up?'

Absolutely not—after their conversation, the previous day, she knew he wouldn't support her.

'No, that's fine. I can handle it. But thanks for the offer.'

'Use the relatives' room,' Iris said with a smile.

'Thanks.'

She took Janine's parents to the relatives' room. 'Can I get you both a cup of tea or coffee?'

Bernie's eyes narrowed. 'No. Don't waste our time. What's all this about?'

'I'm sorry, I don't know your names—I assume they're not the same as Janine's as she says you're her stepfather, Mr…?'

He glowered at her. 'Seeley.'

'Thank you.' She paused. 'I know you want her to give the baby up for adoption, Mr Seeley, but Janine wants to keep him.'

'It's completely out of the question,' he said firmly. 'She's already made one mistake. I'm not going to let her make it worse by keeping the brat.'

Stephanie sighed inwardly. Clearly he wasn't going to give Janine's mum the chance to get a word in edgeways. She was going to have to appeal to his better nature and hope that, beneath the bluster, he had one. 'Would I be right in thinking you were in the police, or maybe the military?'

He bridled. 'What's that got to do with anything?'

'Because your training teaches you to act when you have all the facts, yes?'

'Yes.' His eyes narrowed again.

'Right now, Mr Seeley, I don't think you have all the facts.'

He scoffed. 'She had a one-night stand with a boy at a party she wasn't supposed to go to. And she didn't tell us she was pregnant until it was too late to get rid of the brat. They're the facts.'

'Not quite all,' she said quietly. 'It wasn't a one-night stand.'

'You mean, she's still seeing the boy?' He looked outraged.

'No. I'm afraid there isn't an easy way to say this, so I apologise for being blunt and not preparing you properly—but you both need to know the truth.' She took a deep breath. 'He forced her.'

Mrs Seeley's hands covered her face, and she gave a distressed moan. 'No! He—no. He couldn't have done that to my baby!'

Stephanie nodded grimly. 'I'm sorry.'

'Why didn't she tell us?' Mrs Seeley asked, looking distressed.

'She didn't think you'd believe her. She knew she'd be in trouble for going to the party when she was grounded. And the boy said he'd deny it. Everyone knew she liked him, so they'd assume she'd made a play for him.'

'I'll kill him,' Mr Seeley said, gritting his teeth.

'I understand you're angry, and I would be too in your shoes. I'd want to kill him, too. But that's not going to help Janine,' Stephanie said quietly. 'And there's something else you should know. She thinks you both despise her as a cheap little tramp. She thinks you don't love her. That's why she didn't tell you. She was too scared about how you'd react. She's worried you're going to throw her out because she's broken all your rules.'

'Oh, God, Bernie, we've let her down,' Mrs Seeley said.

He was utterly still. 'Scared? Is she saying I'd hit her?'

'No. But remember, she's still young. Just sixteen. And frightened.'

He frowned. 'And far too young to be a mum. Far too young.'

'Maybe.' Stephanie spread her hands. 'Or maybe, if she gets the right support, it'll be the making of her.'

'Why are you doing this?' Mr Seeley asked, shaking his head. 'Why are you—well, speaking up for her?'

'Because I know someone who went through something similar. They didn't let her keep the baby. And it broke her.' She took a deep breath. 'I wouldn't want to see that happen to someone else.'

The strength of her feelings must have shown in her face, because Mrs Seeley nodded. 'She really wants to keep the baby, even after what the father did to her?'

'That's not the baby's fault,' Stephanie said gently. 'You might not want to hear this, but I think you need to know how Janine feels. She thinks the baby is the only one who's going to love her for herself.'

'But—that's not true. She's my daughter. Of course I love her,' Mrs Seeley said, looking distraught.

'Maybe she needs to hear you say that.' Words that *she* would so have longed to hear from her own mother. But neither of them had had the chance.

'I— She's my daughter, too,' Mr Seeley said. 'I know it's difficult. I'm used to soldiers, not teenage girls.'

So she'd been right in her guess about the military background.

'Janine and I never really got on since Gail and I first got together.' He shrugged. 'I put it down to jealousy.'

'There probably was an element of that,' Stephanie agreed. 'But at the end of the day she's still only sixteen. She's at a really vulnerable age. She needs to know she's loved. She's made a mistake and paid a really heavy price for it, but she needs to know you'll still support her because you're her family.'

'You're right,' Mrs Seeley said. 'And I feel terrible that

it's taken a stranger to tell me what I should've known for myself.'

'Sometimes,' Stephanie said, 'it's a lot easier to talk to a stranger. Someone who doesn't know you, and who doesn't have an emotional stake in the situation.' She thought wryly, how true it had been of her own situation when her marriage to Joe had imploded.

'We've got a spare room,' Mr Seeley said. 'A baby doesn't need a lot of space.'

'It'll mean broken nights. You might wake up when the baby cries.' Mrs Seeley looked anxious.

'They learn to sleep through, soon enough.' He shrugged. 'A grandchild. Grand*son*,' he corrected himself.

So he'd noticed that much. Stephanie smiled to herself. There would be arguments. Bernie Seeley would still lay down the law. But it looked as if he was going to be on Janine's side—and the teenager would get the love and support she wanted so desperately. From a really unexpected quarter.

'Would you like to go and see her now?' Stephanie asked.

'Yes. Yes, we would. Very much,' Mrs Seeley said. 'And— and our grandson.'

She took the Seeleys through to see Janine and lingered just long enough to see Gail hug her and Bernie scoop the baby out of the crib. She smiled and left them to it. They were going to need to do a lot of talking, but she really thought they had a chance of making it now.

'Dan, Harmony's waters have just broken and I need you to check something for me,' Iris said.

Daniel had worked with the senior midwife for long enough to realise that something serious had just happened. 'Sure,' he said, keeping his voice calm for the mum's sake.

A quick examination showed him that the umbilical cord had slipped through before the baby, and the baby's head was pressing against it, cutting off the blood and oxygen supply.

'Harmony, I don't want you to worry,' he said, 'but I need you to turn round on the bed right now, so you're facing the bed, your knees are tucked under, and your bottom is right up in the air.'

'What's happened?'

As he helped her to move round, he explained, 'The umbilical cord has slipped forward before the baby, so we're going to need to give you a Caesarean section. And this isn't going to be too comfortable for you, but until we get you into Theatre Iris is going to push her hand against the baby's head and keep him back there, so the baby can still get the right blood and oxygen supply.'

'Is my baby all right?' Harmony's voice was almost a squeak of panic.

'That's why we're going to deliver him now, to give him the best chance,' Daniel said. 'I know this is scary for you, but I've seen this before and the baby has been just fine. So try not to worry, OK?' He squeezed her hand, and went to the door to call the nearest midwife. 'Can you bleep the anaesthetist for me? I need an emergency section in Theatre One, right now. And I need someone from Paediatrics there when I deliver the baby.'

Knowing his luck, it would be Stephanie; but they were going to have to ignore the slight awkwardness that had sprung up between them since he'd talked to her about keeping a professional distance from Janine.

'I'm on it,' Paula said, and went straight to the phone.

* * *

Stephanie picked up the phone. 'Paediatrics, Stephanie Scott.'

'Stephanie, it's Paula in Maternity. We need you in Theatre One, right now, please,' Paula said. 'We have a mum with a prolapsed cord.'

Stephanie knew what that meant: a compromised blood and oxygen supply, so the baby was going to need resuscitating.

Hopefully the surgeon would be Theo Petrakis. Or anyone rather than Daniel. But if it was Daniel, she'd just have to put her personal feelings aside. The mum and baby were the important ones here. 'I'm on my way,' she said.

As soon as she'd scrubbed up and walked into the theatre, she recognised the surgeon—even gowned and masked, his blue eyes were unmistakeable.

She gave him a wary nod, which he returned.

Once the baby had been delivered, he was handed straight to her. 'Can someone take paired cord blood samples for me while I check him over, please?' she asked.

Just as she'd expected, the baby's Apgar score wasn't brilliant. His airways weren't clear, so she suctioned his mouth and then his nose, to make sure he didn't swallow anything. Then she dried him and tapped his feet to stimulate his breathing, but an assessment of his colour and the way he gasped definitely meant that he needed oxygen. She gave him warmed oxygen and checked his heart rate.

'I'm not happy,' she said to Iris. Especially when she checked his breathing rate; even on one hundred per cent oxygen, his breathing rate was too fast. 'I'm going to start chest compressions. Can you bag him for me?'

She wasn't going to lose this baby. No way was she going to let a mother come round after an emergency section only to discover that she'd lost her baby.

'Come on, little one, you can do this,' she crooned.

Between them, she and Iris continued to resuscitate him. She could see his skin starting to change colour. Please, please let this work. 'He's starting to pink up,' she said.

And then, to her relief, the baby finally began to cry.

'We're there,' Iris said softly.

His Apgar score still wasn't brilliant, but he was getting there.

Three minutes later, they had a crying baby who was breathing for himself.

'Thanks, Iris,' she said.

'Hey. It wasn't just me,' the midwife said.

Daniel came over to join them. 'Well done.'

She gave him a cool nod. 'It's my job.'

'I know, but I'm just glad you're so good at it.'

Considering he'd lectured her on getting too involved with a patient, she wasn't so sure he believed she was good at her job.

'We're on the same page, you know,' he said softly, and let the baby's fist curl round his finger.

She wasn't sure what disarmed her more: the expression on his face as he looked at the baby, or the words he'd just said.

Maybe he'd had a point when he'd warned her not to get too involved. Maybe she'd overreacted because she'd still remembered the way Joe had told her what to do all the time, and she'd tarred Daniel with the same brush. Which was unfair. 'I guess,' she said, and let the baby's other fist curl round her finger.

When Harmony came round from the anaesthetic, Stephanie and Daniel were both there to tell her the good news. 'I do want to keep the baby in the neonatal department for a couple of hours, just to help with his breathing,' Stephanie warned.

'So the cord thing—it didn't… He's all right?'

She knew what Harmony was trying not to put into words. 'He's doing fine. We did have to resuscitate him, but I have to do that with a lot of babies—it just means he had a bit of a tricky start. But he's up on the neonatal ward now and you can visit him any time you like to see him and give him a cuddle.'

A tear trickled down Harmony's cheek. 'Thank you. Both of you.' She looked at Daniel and Stephanie. 'If it hadn't been for you…'

'Try not to think about it,' Daniel said gently. 'Everything's fine now.'

'I'd um, better get back to Paediatrics,' Stephanie said, and made a swift exit.

The next day, at the start of her lunch break, Stephanie called in to see Janine, who seemed a lot happier. 'I'm going home today.'

So the Seeleys hadn't thrown her out.

'Mum and Bernie changed their minds. They're going to let me keep the baby. Bernie says he can talk to school and work out how I can do my exams.'

'That's great,' Stephanie said, meaning it.

'Thank you for helping. Without you, I don't know what I would've done.'

'That's what I'm here for. I'm so pleased it's working out for you.' She gave Janine a hug.

'I'm going to call him Peter Bernard. I think Bernie's pleased. Mum's thrilled.' She gave Stephanie a shy smile. 'I know she would've wanted things to be different for me, but we're going to make the best of it. I think she's OK about being a gran.'

'That's great.' Stephanie squeezed her hand. 'I've got a meeting now, and I probably won't get a chance to see you again before you go to say goodbye, but I'm so glad it's working out.'

'You've been brilliant. Thank you so much.'

'My pleasure.'

And now it was time for her to build a bridge. She dropped by Daniel's office, and knocked on the door. 'Hi.' She could see that he was knee-deep in paperwork. 'I was going to suggest lunch, but…' She gestured at the paperwork on his desk.

'I'm surprised you'd ask.'

She took a deep breath. 'That was the other thing. I owe you an apology. I thought it might be easier to make it over a sandwich.'

'You don't have to apologise. I probably owe you an apology, actually. I'm not your boss. I don't have the right to call you on something.'

'As a colleague,' she said, 'then, yes, you do have the right to call me on something if you think my judgement's wrong.'

'OK. So we're both in the wrong,' he said lightly. 'Is that offer of a sandwich still open?'

Could it really be that easy? 'Sure.'

He glanced out of the window. 'It's pouring, so I guess this means the canteen.'

They managed to get a quiet table in the canteen and sat down.

'OK. My apology. You got Janine talking when none of us could,' Daniel said, 'and you sorted things out so she can keep the baby. What did you say to Janine's parents to talk them round?'

Stephanie brought him up to speed with what Janine

had told her. 'I just put them in the picture so they knew what really happened.'

'That poor kid.' He looked shocked, then angry. 'If anyone ever laid a hand on my daughter…'

'You'd take him apart, I know,' she said. 'I think Bernie Seeley would like to do that to the boy concerned, but violence really isn't the way to solve things.'

'No, I guess not.' He paused. 'You're good with words. You've made a real difference to their lives.'

'I hope so. I think they've got a better chance of being able to build a real family relationship, now they're talking and being open with each other.'

He smiled at her. 'Days when you get a chance to make a difference like that are really good, aren't they?'

'Absolutely. They make all the paperwork and the tough days worthwhile.' She didn't have to elaborate on that, because she knew he'd know exactly what she meant: days when you lost a patient or couldn't make a difference. 'And I'm sorry, too. You did have a point about needing to keep a professional distance.'

'Any reason why you found it hard in Janine's case?' he asked lightly.

Yes. Her own mother. Not that she wanted to tell him about that. 'Empathy,' she hedged.

'Fair enough.' He paused. 'I enjoyed our date.'

'Me, too.'

'I know we got off on the wrong foot again, just now, but I wondered if you'd like to come out with me again?'

She ought to be sensible and refuse; she knew that she was hopeless at relationships. But something about Daniel drew her. He was the first man since Joe that she'd actually wanted to get to know better. Maybe, she thought, she should give this another try. 'OK.' She paused. 'How about one of the medical museums? The one with the operating theatre?'

He smiled. 'I've always wanted to go there. When?'

'I'm on a late, next Monday morning.'

He checked his diary. 'That works for me. We can have lunch afterwards. Shall I meet you there straight after the school run?'

'Sure.' And she tried not to think about how much she was looking forward to it.

CHAPTER SEVEN

STEPHANIE WAS GLAD she was working over the weekend, because she knew she would've been antsy if she'd been stuck at home, thinking about her date with Daniel. On the Monday morning she changed her outfit three times before telling herself how ridiculous she was, especially as they were both going to work afterwards and no way could she turn up at work for a late shift on the children's ward looking glitzy. She changed back into the sensible black trousers and three-quarter-sleeved jersey top she normally wore at work.

Although it was the end of September, it was still warm enough outside for her not to need a coat. And she couldn't wait to see Daniel.

They'd agreed to meet outside the museum. She was there first. And it was weird how her stomach felt as if it was filled with butterflies. They were supposed to be taking this slowly, seeing where it took them. So she really shouldn't make such a big deal out of it.

And, actually, she felt vaguely foolish waiting outside for him. Like a teenager on a blind date, wondering if he'd be there or if he'd stand her up.

She was even crosser with herself when her heart felt as if it had just done a backflip when she caught sight of

Daniel walking down the road towards her and he raised his hand in greeting.

'Sorry I'm late,' he said. 'Mia's teacher wanted a quick word and then there was a delay on the Tube. Have you been waiting long?'

It had felt like for ever. 'No, it's fine.'

He kissed her cheek. 'You look lovely.'

She laughed. 'Daniel, we're both on a late shift. I'm wearing exactly what I normally wear for work.'

'Exactly.'

She frowned, not following. 'What?'

'You look lovely,' he said again. 'Just as you do at work.'

'Oh.' The compliment warmed her from the inside out. 'Thank you.'

'I'm not trying to soft-soap you, either.'

'I know.' She placed her hand on his arm for a second, just so he'd know she appreciated it.

'Shall we go up?' he asked, gesturing for her to go first.

She made her way up the narrow spiral steps into the old museum. She enjoyed walking with Daniel through the herb garret where the apothecaries used to store their supplies, and looking in the display cases at some of the medical instruments doctors in their positions would've had to use years ago.

'Scary stuff. Imagine trying to talk a child into this now,' she said, gesturing to the leeches.

'I don't think you could talk me into it, either,' Daniel said with a grimace.

They made their way to the theatre itself.

'I didn't expect it to be like this,' Stephanie said. 'It's like an actual theatre, with that narrow wooden operating table as a stage and that horseshoe-shaped stand for onlookers.'

'And of course they didn't have electricity, so they had

to rely on the skylight to help them see what they were doing,' Daniel said.

'I'm really glad we didn't have to learn like this as students.' She glanced up at the sign on the wall. 'Look, only the apprentices and dressers of the surgeon could stand around the table and really see what he was doing. The front row was reserved for the dressers of other surgeons, and the last three rows were for pupils.'

'And visitors were allowed by the surgeon's permission. I suppose you were bound to get rich patrons wanting to see what the surgeon did with their money,' he said.

'Probably. And I take it the dressers were the assistants?'

'The ones who sorted out the dressings and tourniquets,' Daniel said. 'And sometimes they had to hold the patients down.'

'I'm so glad we've moved beyond that.' She grimaced. 'Anaesthetic and antiseptic—what would we do without them?'

'A lot less than we do now,' he said. 'It would've been too dangerous to do internal operations.'

'And they had no idea about antiseptic, back when this theatre was first used. They might not even have wiped the surgical tools between patients,' she said.

'No wonder so many women died of puerperal fever.' He shivered. 'It doesn't bear thinking about. I'm so glad we don't have to work in those conditions now.'

She glanced through the brochure. 'They were fast, though. It says they could do amputations and sew up the stump in less than a minute, though they had to give patients alcohol or opiates to numb them first.' She bit her lip. 'Oh, those poor patients.'

'It makes me appreciate the tools of my trade a lot more,' Daniel said.

Afterwards, they had just enough time to grab lunch before their shift.

'I really enjoyed today,' Daniel said. 'Maybe we can go somewhere else next week?'

'I'd like that. We can sort out a date later.'

'Sure.' He smiled at her. 'We'd better get to the hospital or we'll be late for our shift.'

They walked in easy silence towards the hospital. When they were two roads away, he stopped.

'Everything OK?' she asked.

'Yes and no.' He wrinkled his nose. 'I want to kiss you goodbye, but if I do that any nearer to the hospital than now, someone's bound to see us and we'll be the hottest topic on the grapevine. I assume you'd rather avoid that.'

It sounded as if he would, too. Was he having second thoughts about their relationship?

The question must have shown in her expression because he said softly, 'Which doesn't mean that I've changed my mind about us, just that I want to keep it strictly between us for now. It's still early days. I don't want Mia hearing gossip and worrying that her life is going to change dramatically.'

Which was fair enough. She relaxed. 'I've been the hottest topic on the grapevine before now and it wasn't pleasant. I'm not sure whether the whispering was the worst, or the pity.'

'Definitely the pity,' he said, sounding heartfelt.

Of course—he must've had to deal with a lot of that after his wife had been killed in the accident. 'Sorry. I didn't mean to be tactless.'

'I know.' He leaned forward and kissed her very lightly on the mouth. Her lips tingled and warmth seemed to spread through her entire body. He pulled back just far enough so they could look into each other's eyes; in answer to the question she saw in his, she gave the tiniest, tiniest nod and leaned towards him.

This time, he slid one arm round her waist, holding her close, and slid one hand behind her neck, cradling her head. Her mouth still tingled, but this time with anticipation as his lips brushed lightly against hers, and then again, and then a third time, when she found her mouth opening beneath his, letting him deepen the kiss.

By the time he broke the kiss, her pulse was racing; she was pretty sure he was just as affected by it, because his pupils were huge and there was a slight flush across his cheekbones.

She traced the slash of colour with the tip of her finger. 'I don't think either of us was quite expecting that,' she said, her voice husky.

'No. And I dare not kiss you again—much as I want to—or we'll end up being arrested.'

His voice was gratifyingly rough, too. And his words made her smile. 'I feel like a teenager.'

'Me, too,' he admitted. 'If we weren't on duty, I'd suggest finding the nearest funfair. Though kissing you gets my heart beating faster than a roller-coaster would.'

'Better than a roller-coaster. Now that's different.' But the compliment pleased her, because she knew it was genuine. 'Dan, we can't bunk off. They're expecting us. We'd be letting the team down.'

'I know. So we're going to walk to the hospital together like professionals,' he said. 'Two colleagues who've just bumped into each other on the street and are chatting on the way to work. And neither of us is going to think about kissing—right?'

'Right.' Though she had a feeling that that might be easier said than done. That kiss had just about fried her brain.

* * *

Over the next couple of weeks, Daniel found himself getting closer to Stephanie. He really hadn't expected it to be so good between them. He liked her sharp mind when it came to work; and she was really good with patients, explaining things clearly yet without patronising them. Working with her was a pleasure.

Outside work, it was even better. He really looked forward to their dates out, and he hadn't expected that, either. For the last four years he'd been protecting his heart from any potential damage by simply not dating and concentrating on bringing up his daughter, but something about Stephanie had drawn him right from the first.

He liked her. He enjoyed spending time with her. She made his heart skip a beat.

Was now the right time for him to move on?

Stephanie was the first woman who'd challenged him out of his comfort zone since Meg's death. The first woman he'd kissed since then. But he had a feeling that she was still holding a lot back from him. Was he expecting too much from her, hoping that she'd fit easily into his life because she'd treated his daughter and Mia had seemed to like her?

And how would the other people in his life react to him moving on? Mia had said she wanted a mum; Lucy had as good as told him that he had her blessing and that of their parents. But what about Meg's parents?

If he wanted to move forward with this—and he was pretty sure that he did—then he needed to talk to them.

On the Friday night, Daniel called in to see the Parkers.

'Is Mia not with you?' Meg's mum, Hestia, asked. 'Is something wrong?'

'No, she's fine. I just wanted to see you on my own,' Daniel said.

She still looked slightly concerned, but asked, 'Would you like some coffee?'

'That would be lovely, thanks, Hestia.' He followed her into the kitchen.

'So what did you want to see us about?' Ben, Meg's father, asked.

The big question. And the only way Daniel could think of to face it was head on. With a little bit of softening; he didn't want to hurt them. 'Um. There isn't really a tactful way to say this. But you know that Meg was the love of my life, don't you?'

Hestia looked at him and raised an eyebrow. 'You've met someone else, haven't you?'

'Ye-es.' Daniel blew out a breath. 'I haven't introduced her to anyone in the family, yet, because it's still early days.'

Ben frowned. 'But she's obviously special enough for you to start thinking about it.'

'Yes, she is.' He sighed. 'You know I'll always think of you as my other parents, and Mia will always be your granddaughter—that won't ever change.'

'But you want our blessing to see someone else,' Ben said.

He'd wanted to talk to them about it. Not to ask for their permission, exactly, but having their blessing would mean a lot to him. 'I'd feel happier if I knew you understood and won't hold it against me, yes,' Daniel admitted.

Hestia came over to him and hugged him. 'Love, you're still young. Thirty-five's no age at all. You've got most of your life ahead of you. Yes, it hurts to think that you're going to replace our Meg, but we always knew this was going to happen someday.'

'I'm not replacing her,' Daniel reassured her swiftly. 'Meg will always be Mia's mum and she'll always have a place in my heart.'

'But you can't spend the rest of your life on your own, being lonely. I know Mia has us, and your parents, and Lucy, but that's not the same as having a mother figure around. Having someone there for her would be good, too.' Hestia paused. 'Does she like children?'

'She's a doctor on the children's ward, so I guess you could say that.' He smiled at them. 'Actually, Mia's already met her once—but only in her professional capacity. She doesn't know we've been seeing each other.'

'Right. Is she the one we made cakes for?' Hestia asked.

Daniel nodded. 'But I wasn't seeing her then. She was simply a colleague. But I admit, I do feel a bit guilty about seeing her.'

'Because of Meg? She wouldn't have wanted you to be lonely. She would've wanted you to have someone to love. Someone who'd love you back,' Hestia said, and Daniel could see the film of tears in her eyes. 'If she makes you happy, then you go ahead, love.'

'You've got our blessing,' Ben added.

Daniel could feel the moisture in his own eyes, and had to blink hard. 'Thank you,' he said, his voice rough with emotion.

'No, thank *you*,' Hestia said. 'You don't have to take our feelings into consideration when it comes to your life.' She patted his arm. 'But Meg was right about you. You're a good man. You care, and you don't just ride roughshod over people.' She paused. 'Actually, I'd already guessed.'

Daniel stared at her, surprised. 'How?'

'Mia drew a picture of you while she was here last. You had the biggest smile ever. I asked her about it, and she said you were really smiley nowadays.'

'I hope I wasn't ever a grumpy dad,' he said lightly. He'd tried so hard not to damage his daughter with his own grief after Meg's death.

'No, I think it was her way of saying that you don't have that sadness in your eyes all the time any more. I know how much you've missed Meg—we all have—and if only that woman…' Hestia sighed and shook her head. 'Well, wishing isn't going to bring Meg back. But seeing you happy again is the next best thing.'

That was the last hurdle for Daniel. He knew his parents and Lucy would accept Stephanie immediately, and he was pretty sure that Mia would get on well with her. Now all he had to do was talk Stephanie into meeting them. He had a feeling that she was antsy about families, and he was pretty sure that it was something to do with her divorce. He hadn't asked because it had felt too much like prying. But maybe now he could persuade her to open up to him.

It was a busy week and time seemed to fly past. Stephanie had two lunch meetings with Daniel, both of them discreet; she found herself relaxing more with him, and she looked forward to his company.

When she confessed that to him, he smiled. 'Me, too. It's been a long time since I've…well, had fun like this. Which doesn't mean I resent Mia—I love my daughter and I don't regret a single second I spend with her.'

'No, I know what you mean—just having a little time you can spend doing something for you and not having to worry about someone else.'

On Wednesday, the following week, they went to the Whispering Gallery at St Paul's cathedral. Daniel smiled at Stephanie. 'Stay there. I'm going to the opposite side of the gallery.'

To her delight, he whispered into the wall—and she heard very clearly what he said. 'I want to kiss you.'

'Dan!' she said, and heard him laugh.

'Listen again, and tell me how many echoes you hear,' he said—and then clapped his hands once.

'Four,' she whispered back. 'Did you read up about it or are you a nerd?'

He came back to join her. 'Guilty on both counts,' he said. 'Let's go up to the next gallery.'

They climbed up to the stone gallery, then finally to the Golden Gallery at the stop, where they had a stunning view over London.

'Look, there's the Globe,' he said, pointing it out to her. 'And the Tate Modern.'

'I don't think I ever realised how wide the river Thames is,' she said. 'What a fantastic view.'

He put his arms protectively round her. 'Know what I'm thinking?' he asked.

She glanced round, noticing that nobody had come up to the Golden Gallery. 'Right now it's just you and me, and we're so far above London that nobody's going to notice us, even if they look up—so you can do what you suggested in the Whispering Gallery.'

'I love it that you're so in tune with me,' he said, and kissed her.

Time seemed to stop. All she was aware of was the warmth of Daniel's body, his arms wrapped round her; the softness of his mouth on hers, teasing and promising; and the way his kiss made her temperature spike.

When he broke the kiss, she felt incredibly hot and bothered.

'OK?' he asked softly.

She nodded, not quite trusting herself to speak.

He stroked her face. 'Do you have any idea how pretty you look when you blush?'

And she felt the colour sweep even more strongly into her face. 'Flatterer,' she muttered.

'No. You're lovely.' He stole another kiss. 'And I guess we ought to go down, before someone else comes up here and finds us behaving like teenagers.'

'I guess.'

'So was it what you expected?' Daniel asked when they left the cathedral and walked back out into the street.

'It was beautiful,' she said. 'Thanks for bringing me.'

'My pleasure.'

They walked hand in hand through the streets, Stephanie couldn't remember when she'd last felt so in tune with someone—even Joe.

But there was the sticking point.

She was going to have to tell Daniel about her past, if they were to have a chance at making a go of things. And it was probably better to do it now—because if it made a difference, the way it had with Joe, at least her heart wouldn't be so involved. If she left it until she'd really fallen in love with Daniel Connor, she'd risk getting seriously hurt.

'Dan, there's something you need to know about me if things are going to go any further between us,' she said.

He looked wary. 'What?'

This was it. The thing that could change everything. She took a deep breath. 'I wasn't brought up in a family. I was brought up in a children's home because my mum wasn't allowed to keep me.'

Instead of backing away, like she'd expected, he kept his fingers laced through hers. 'So is this why you stood up for Janine like that?'

She nodded. 'I guess it hit a raw spot with me. My mum was about the same age as Janine when she was pregnant with me. Her parents threw her out when they found out she was expecting.'

'What about your dad?'

'I've no idea—he's not named on my birth certificate.' She swallowed hard. 'I hope he loved her and it just went wrong between them because they were both too young to cope with what was happening. I'd really hate to think that what happened to Janine happened to her, too.'

'That's pretty tough on you. I understand now why you wanted to talk Janine's parents round.' He paused. 'What happened to your mum? Did you manage to get back in touch with her when you were older?'

She closed her eyes for a moment. 'My mum didn't cope very well on her own. There wasn't the kind of support back then that you get nowadays. I was taken away from her when I was about two. I can just about remember her being allowed to come and see me at the children's home, some weekends. I remember a lady with a pretty flowery dress and she smelled of roses—and then she stopped coming to see me.' She looked away. 'I learned years later that she'd taken an overdose. She couldn't cope with me being taken away from her.'

Daniel wrapped his arms round her. 'That's so sad. Poor woman. She never got the chance to be with you and see you grow up.'

Just like his wife hadn't had the chance to see Mia grow up.

Of course Daniel would understand. He'd sort of been there himself. She should've thought of that before. 'Sorry. I didn't mean to rip the top off your scars.'

'You haven't.' He held her closer.

'I wish I'd known my mum. Or that her parents had looked after her properly.' She had to blink the tears away. 'Sorry, I didn't mean to spoil our date.'

'Not at all. I can't imagine what it would be like to grow up without my family. Dad and I only ever talk about football—typical bloke stuff—but I know if I was in trouble I could talk to him about anything. The same with my mum and my sister.' He paused. 'So you weren't adopted?'

'I guess I slipped through the cracks—and then I was too old.' Not that Joe's family had ever understood that. They'd made her feel as if she was unlovable, as if there had been something lacking in her. 'The thing is, most people want a baby; they don't want to foster or adopt a stroppy teen. Though I was lucky. My best friend at school was great and her family let me live with them in the sixth form so I could do my A levels. They're pretty much the nearest I have to a family, though obviously I'm not actually related to them. Well, not unless you count me being godmother to Trish's son.'

'I'm glad you had someone.' He held her tighter. 'What about your grandparents? Did you ever try to find them?'

'Yes. I found them when I was eighteen. After I'd done my A levels and I knew I had a place at university to study medicine.' She sighed. 'I had this stupid idea they might be proud of me. But they just didn't want to know me. They didn't even invite me indoors. The just said they weren't interested and shut the front door in my face.'

'More fool them,' he said.

'I'm not upset about it, Dan. I'm glad. I didn't want to be a family with people who were so bigoted and unkind.' She thought, I married into one that was nearly as bad—but at least I'm out of it now.

She shook herself. 'Anyway, it's all in the past now. They're both dead. I don't have anyone related to me in the world—at least, nobody I know of—but I don't actually need a family. I have good friends and a job I love.'

And that was enough. It had to be. 'Now, I'll stop being maudlin. Let's go for an ice cream.'

'You're not being maudlin. You're brave and you're strong, and I love that instead of being bitter about life you've focused on the good stuff. I'm proud to know you,' he said.

It made her feel warm inside. And scared, at the same time. Taking things further between them meant taking a risk. She'd shared this much with Daniel; she wasn't ready yet to tell him about what had happened with Joe, but so far he'd seemed to understand. It was a good start.

CHAPTER EIGHT

DANIEL RAISED HIS eyebrows when he met Stephanie outside the canteen for their weekly project liaison meeting. 'You look terrible,' he said.

She grimaced. 'Let's say it's been a bit of a rough morning in the PAU.'

'Want to talk about it?'

She sighed. 'It's something I have to deal with. I shouldn't burden you with my casework.'

He spread his hands. 'Hey, you're a doctor, not a superhero—and we've all had days where we've needed to offload to someone. Tell me.'

She bit her lip. 'I had a case this morning where a baby came in with a broken leg—a spiral fracture, after he rolled off a changing mat.'

'It happens,' he said dryly. 'You think the baby can't roll yet and you turn away for a matter of seconds to get a nappy or a baby wipe or something you've forgotten, and in that tiny, tiny space of time the baby rolls over for the first time and goes straight off the changing mat to the floor.'

'That sounds like experience talking.'

'And how.' He rolled his eyes. 'Luckily, the changing mat was on the floor at the time rather than the changing station,' he said, 'or I would've been there beating myself up about not looking after the baby properly. I imagine the parents were pretty upset about it.'

'The mum was, yes—the dad didn't come in with her. But the social worker thinks it wasn't an accident, especially as it wasn't the only fracture.'

He looked surprised. 'The baby had more than one fracture?'

'No, there's an older brother—he came in with them—and he had a cast on. It seems he ended up with a broken arm last month.'

He winced. 'Nasty. So the social worker thinks it's abuse?'

She nodded.

'But you don't?'

'Dan, you know as well as I do that abuse isn't the only reason for fractures. Yes, it's a possibility, but my gut instinct tells me there's more to this case than that. The family lives in a high-rise flat and the lift is always broken, so it's hard for the mum to get out with pram and a toddler.'

'Which means it can be frustrating, being cooped up all day.'

She could see exactly where he was going with that. 'And then the mother took out the frustration on the baby, shook the children maybe and caused the fractures?' She spread her hands. 'Maybe. But it's not the only possibility, Dan. Being stuck indoors means not getting enough sunlight, and that mean not enough vitamin D is being produced in the body.'

'Rickets?' he said.

'It's a possibility. Soft bones means more likelihood of fractures.'

'There any a few other possible genetic problems,' he said. 'Are there any signs of anything in the mum?'

'I was more focused on treating the baby,' she admitted. 'Actually, you might even know the mum, as she had the baby here at the London Victoria. Her name's Della Goldblum.'

Daniel looked thoughtful. 'Yes, I remember her—if I'm right, I think her mum was looking after her toddler while she was in hospital having the baby and a friend was her birth partner. Isn't her partner in prison?'

She nodded. 'The social worker says it's for GBH. He hasn't seen the baby yet, so he wasn't the cause of either of the fractures, though the social worker was pretty quick to suggest it.'

'Do you think he hits Della when he's out of prison?'

'I don't know.' She bit her lip. 'But the social worker suspects it and she wants both children taken into care. We're keeping the baby in on the ward while we run some tests. Della's only allowed in to see the baby if someone's there to supervise her.' She grimaced. 'It's a horrible situation.'

'It keeps the children safe, though, while the tests are being run,' he pointed out gently.

'I know, and I know there are way too many cases when children slip through the net and the abuse is missed. We don't want that to happen to the Goldblum children.' She shivered. 'I know we're taking the cautious route and it's the right thing to do, but at the same time my gut instinct is telling me that Della Goldblum isn't a baby-batterer. Dan, would the ultrasound pictures of the baby still be on file?'

'Yes.'

'Maybe I need to review them. They might show symptoms we're missing at the moment. Maybe there's some bowing of the long bones, or the skull might not be so clear on the ultrasound, because decreased echogenicity of the bones means that the sound waves won't bounce properly off the surface.'

'You're thinking osteogenesis imperfecta?' he asked.

'It's another possibility. Obviously we're not going to rule out abuse just yet, but I think we need to check any possible medical conditions that affect the bones as well. I'm going to start with vitamin D deficiency and take it from there.'

'I don't want to burst your bubble, but if there were any signs of OI on the prenatal scans,' he said, 'then I'm pretty sure the sonographer would've picked it up and flagged it with the midwife or the consultant.'

She sighed. 'Yes, you're right. Sorry, I'm not thinking straight—and I shouldn't let myself get this involved. I need to keep a professional distance.'

'Good idea,' he said. 'But if there's anything you think I can do to help, let me know. Remember the departmental liaison thing works both ways.'

'Thanks. I appreciate that.' And she appreciated that he'd listened to her rather than dismissing her concerns. Joe had never wanted to hear about her job, saying that she ought to leave her cases at work and not think about them when she was home. But what doctor could cut herself off completely like that?

When the test results came back, the next day, Stephanie reviewed them and her heart sank. No sign of vitamin D deficiency. She'd reviewed the prenatal scans, too; and, just as Daniel had warned, they were clear.

Her patients kept her too busy to brood about it during her shift, but she couldn't stop thinking about the case on the way home and wondering what she was missing. She texted Daniel when she got in.

Seems I was wrong about rickets. Nothing on the prenatal scans, either.

Five minutes later, his name flashed up on the screen of her phone. 'Are you OK?' he asked when she answered.

'Yes,' she lied.

'You don't sound it.'

'I'll live.'

'Do you want me to come over?' he asked softly.

Yes. Right now, she could really do with a hug. But she also knew she was being totally selfish. 'I can't ask you to do that. You have Mia to think about.'

'You could come here,' he suggested.

'No—that's not fair to her. What if she wakes up, comes downstairs and sees me in the house? She's going to ask questions, and neither of us is ready to give those answers yet.'

'You're right,' he said, and sighed. 'Stephanie, try not to brood about it. You've done what you can.'

'I know, I know—and professional detachment is important.' Though it was easier said than done. Some cases just stayed with you and you couldn't ignore them. 'Thanks for listening, Dan.'

'Any time.'

An hour later, Stephanie's doorbell rang. She frowned. Who would call at this time of night? She picked up the entryphone. 'Hello?'

'Stephanie? It's Dan. Can I come up?'

Dan? What was he doing here? 'What about Mia?'

'Don't worry. My sister's babysitting. That's why I was so long; I needed to wait for Lucy to come over, first.'

She pressed the buzzer to let him in, and met him at her front door.

He handed her a tub of premium ice cream. 'I think you might need this.'

'Thank you.' She gave him a rueful smile. 'I didn't mean for you to come rushing over.'

'Think nothing of it. You're concerned about your patient. It always help to talk it out.' He gave her a hug.

And how much better that made her feel.

'I hope you were intending to share this with me,' she said.

He grinned. 'That was the plan.'

She fetched two spoons, and enjoyed sharing the entire tub with him.

Afterwards, they lay together on her sofa, their arms wrapped round each other. She looked up at him. Was he going to kiss her? And, given that this time they weren't in a public place, would the kiss turn hotter? Would he touch her?

The tips of her fingers tingled; right now, she really wanted to touch him.

On every date they'd been on, he'd been dressed for work in a suit and tie. She'd seen him in scrubs in Theatre, but tonight was the first time she'd seen him in jeans and a T-shirt. And he was utterly gorgeous.

She looked at his mouth. There was the tiniest smear of ice cream against his lips, and couldn't resist reaching up and touching it with the tip of her tongue.

He shivered. 'Stephanie.'

'Ice cream,' she said.

He ran the tip of his forefinger along her mouth. 'I can't see any ice cream here.'

'Oh, there is,' she said with a grin. 'You're using the wrong sense.'

'Am I, now?' he asked, his pupils growing larger.

'Yes,' she whispered.

Then he bent his head to kiss her. Tiny, teasing kisses that brushed against her mouth and made every nerve end sing into life. Her control splintered and she opened her mouth, letting him deepen the kiss.

He slid his hands under her T-shirt, splaying his palms against her back, and it gave her the courage to do the same. His skin was so soft, so smooth. And suddenly none of this was enough; she needed more. She moved her fingertips against his skin in tiny circles, urging him on.

In response, he let one hand glide round to her midriff, stroking her skin, and gradually moved his hand upwards. She arched against him as his other hand released the catch of her bra, and then at last she felt his fingers where she needed them, caressing the undersides of her breasts and teasing her nipples.

She could feel his erection pressing against her, and knew he wanted this as much as she did. The need to be closer to him spiralled, and she broke the kiss. 'Dan. Take me to bed,' she invited.

He groaned and kissed her lightly. 'Stephanie, I wasn't expecting this to happen between us tonight. I haven't got any condoms.' His voice was husky with frustration and need.

'You don't need them,' she said. 'I'm on the Pill—not for contraception, but because my periods are horrible without it.' She dragged in a breath. 'Just so you know, I haven't slept with anyone except my ex for the last few years.'

'And I haven't slept with anyone at all since Meg died, four years ago,' he said. He kissed her lightly. 'It's your call. Are you OK with this?'

She knew he meant more than just worries about pregnancy and disease: was she ready to make love with him, after all this time of being on her own? And Dan was facing the same kind of pressure, if not more—because he at least had loved his wife until Meg had been taken from him, whereas she and Joe had fallen out of love with each other and the end of their marriage had been miserable for both of them.

'I am if you are,' she said.

He smiled. 'I'm very OK.' He kissed her again.

She wasn't quite sure which of them moved first, but then they were on their feet, and he'd scooped her into his arms. Panic skittered through her. Was she doing the right thing? Was this too soon? Would she even remember how to do this?

'Forgive me. I'm having a bit of a caveman moment,' he said, his eyes crinkling at the corners.

And suddenly all her worries dissolved. This was Dan. Everything was going to be all right. She laughed. 'Troglodyte is good.'

'Where's your room?' he asked.

'Next door.'

He carried her out of the living room. He managed to open her bedroom door without dropping her, then slowly lowered her to her feet so her body was pressed against his.

'Are you quite sure about this?' he asked.

'Oh, I'm sure.' She reached up to kiss him.

'Good. Because if we don't do something about this right now, I think I'm going to spontaneously combust.'

'The troglodyte discovers fire?' she teased.

'Oh, and just for that, Stephanie Scott...' He tugged at the hem of her T-shirt and she lifted her arms to let him peel the soft cotton over her head. He'd already undone her lacy bra earlier and it fell to the floor, exposing her to his view.

He sucked in a breath. 'You're beautiful, Stephanie.'

She could feel her skin heating and her body responding to his.

He kissed the curve of her neck, and traced a path of

kisses along her collarbones. Then he dropped to his knees and kissed a path down her sternum, over her abdomen.

She shivered and he undid the button of her jeans, slowly lowered the zip and stroked the material down over her hips until her jeans fell to the floor.

She stepped out of them, not wanting to fall over and make an idiot of herself, breaking the mood. She stood with her hands on her hips; eyes narrowed, she surveyed him. 'You're a bit overdressed now,' she said.

'What do you suggest?' he asked.

She pursed her lips. 'You could always take your clothes off for me.'

He stilled momentarily before speedily peeling off his T-shirt.

Stephanie stifled a gasp. Dan was gorgeous. A perfect six-pack. Even though she doubted he had the time to work out at a gym, he hadn't just let himself go to seed.

'You're beautiful, Dan,' she said softly.

'So are you.' He dropped his T-shirt. 'How about you finish this, Stephanie? Because right now I really need to feel your hands on me.'

Her thoughts exactly. Her hands were shaking as she lowered the zip of his jeans. She stroked his abdomen, enjoying the feel of his musculature, then peeled the denim down.

He stepped out of his jeans, then drew her close and kissed her hard. 'You're absolutely, absolutely sure about this?'

No. She was terrified that she was going to make an idiot of herself. 'Yes,' she lied.

'OK.' He pulled her duvet back, lifted her up and laid her gently against the pillows. He knelt between her thighs and stayed there for a moment, just looking at her. 'You're so beautiful, Stephanie.' He stroked her midriff. 'Your skin's so soft.' He let his hands slide up to cup her breasts. 'And you're so responsive.'

She shivered. 'You're beautiful, too—and I want you, Dan. I really want you. Right here, right now.'

He leaned forward to kiss her lightly, then kissed his way down her abdomen. She shivered again as he slid one finger under the lacy trim of her knickers. He gently pushed one finger inside her and moved his thumb to tease her clitoris.

She shuddered and he stopped. 'OK?' he checked.

'Very OK.' Her voice had practically dropped an octave, she was so turned on.

But he didn't tease her about it, to her relief; he simply kissed her lightly. 'Good.' He kept stroking her, and the pleasure coiled tighter and tighter.

Then Stephanie stopped thinking at all as her body convulsed round him.

He held her until the aftershocks had died down.

'Thank you— I…' She grimaced. 'Sorry, I'm a bit incoherent.'

He chuckled and stole a kiss. 'You don't know what that does to my ego, knowing that I've reduced such a clever woman to mush like this.'

'Um.' She didn't know what to say. 'Thank you.'

'My pleasure.' He stroked her hair back from her face. 'I wanted the first time to be for you.'

When had someone last been so considerate of her feelings? Certainly not Joe. It brought her close to tears; to hide her emotion, she kissed him and explored his body until his breathing went shallow and he was shaking.

'Now?' she asked.

'Yes.' The word came out as a hiss of need.

He shifted to kneel between her thighs. The tip of his penis nudged against her.

And then slowly, sweetly, he slid deep inside her. He stayed still, letting her adjust to the weight of his body; then, finally, he began to move, holding her close as he pushed deeper.

His lovemaking was warm and sweet and slow, and Stephanie really hadn't expected it to be like this—sweet and sharp at the same time. She was shockingly aware of another climax building; was it simply that her body had been so starved for pleasure, it was making up for lost time? Or was it because it was Dan making love with her?

Her body tightened around his, tipping him into his own climax, and as her heart rate slowed to normal she was aware of the tears spilling down her cheeks.

'Stephanie? Are you OK?' he asked, looking worried

'More than OK,' she whispered. 'It's been a long time. I wasn't expecting this to be so good. To—well…' She blushed, and was cross with herself. How could she be shy with him after what they'd just done?

'Me, too.' He kissed her gently. 'Stephanie. I feel horrible about this, as if I've just got what I wanted and now I'm deserting you, but I—' He dragged in a breath. 'Much as I'd like to, I'm sorry, I can't stay with you tonight.'

'Of course you can't,' she said. Did he really think she didn't know that? 'You have Mia to think about, and you can't expect your sister to stay babysit all night. You've probably already been longer than you said you'd be.' And that was all her fault, for being needy.

'Thank you for understanding.' He kissed her again. 'Next time—oh, hell, that makes it sound as if I'm taking you for granted, and I don't mean that. Just that you and I, we're good together, and I'd like to do this again.'

'Me, too,' she admitted. And hearing him sound all flustered made her feel so much better.

'Next time,' he said, 'my timing's going to be better. And I won't have to rush off.'

'It's OK. Really it is,' she said.

He smiled and stole another kiss. 'Stay there—you look comfortable. I'll see myself out.'

'OK.' She watched him dressing. Daniel was beautiful, and she was still amazed by how he'd given her so much pleasure. Whatever happened between them in the future, they'd had this. And he'd made her feel wonderful. Special. *Cherished.*

He kissed her goodbye. 'See you tomorrow, honey. Sweet dreams.'

'You, too.' And they would be sweet, she knew, thanks to him.

CHAPTER NINE

'I CAN'T BELIEVE they've got Christmas cards for sale in the hospital shop,' Daniel said. 'It's still only October!'

'There's wrapping, tinsel and tree decorations in the supermarket, too,' Stephanie told him dryly. 'There's no escape.'

He sighed. 'I shouldn't be so bah humbug about it all. It's lovely having babies on the ward at Christmas.'

'But?' she asked, seeing the doubts in his expression.

'Christmas is always bitter-sweet for me,' he said. 'If I didn't have Mia, I'd probably go abroad somewhere to avoid it.'

She waited, knowing there was more.

Eventually, he raked his hand through his hair and told her. 'Meg's accident was at the beginning of December,' he said. 'That year, Mia was the only thing that kept me going. I had to face it for her sake and make the day special for her.'

But inside his heart had been breaking. She'd just bet he'd had as many sympathy cards as Christmas cards that year. And how hard it must've been to celebrate Christmas when he'd had a funeral to plan.

Christmas, birthdays and anniversaries were always tough when you'd lost someone, she knew. Or when you didn't have a family to make the days special for you;

even if you had good friends to celebrate the good times with you, there was still something missing. A family-shaped hole.

He'd shared something tough with her. Maybe it was her turn to let him know he wasn't alone. 'Actually, I know what you mean,' she said. 'I, um—my marriage finally broke up just before Christmas.' And it was the anniversary of the miscarriage next month: a day she always found hard, even though the baby had never been hers. 'It's a tough time of year.'

'Break-ups are never easy,' he agreed, 'but Christmas always makes things harder.'

She shrugged. 'There was one plus point. I didn't have to spend Christmas with Joe's family that year.'

Given what Stephanie had told him about growing up in care, Daniel was pretty sure that Christmas had always been hard for her. And it sounded as if she hadn't found the family she'd been hoping for when she'd got married.

Something in her expression warned him not to ask any more. So, instead, he said lightly, 'Not all in-laws are difficult, you know.'

'I guess not.' Though she didn't look convinced.

'Mine are nice.'

'Your in-laws or your family?'

'Both,' he said. 'Actually, my in-laws are very much part of my family.'

She looked surprised. 'Even though…?'

'Meg's dead? Yes. Mia's still their granddaughter. And I'm still their son-in-law. That's not going to change, even if I see someone else. Even if…' He paused. No. It was too early to talk about a future. She hadn't even met his family, yet. And it sounded as if she had real issues about families. As if she found them painful. This could end up being a sticking point in their relationship.

Right now, he needed to lighten their moods. 'Well. I hope you're prepared for Christmas on the children's ward.'

'If it's anything like it was in Manchester,' she said, 'we'll have a huge tree, the Friends of the Hospital will have bought and wrapped a little gift for every child and every sibling, and someone's going to be Father Christmas to deliver them—my guess is that it'll be Rhys.'

'Don't forget the sausage rolls and mince pies,' he said. 'Parents bring them in by the plateful. And tins of chocolate biscuits.'

'Good. I love chocolate biscuits.'

He smiled. 'I'll remember that.'

She smiled back. 'I'd better get back. I have clinic in ten minutes.'

'Yeah. I'll call you later,' he said. On days when they weren't going to get the chance to see each other, they'd fallen into the habit of chatting on the phone. At the same time that he enjoyed it, it also made him feel antsy; was getting close to Stephanie the right thing to do? Could they overcome each other's doubts and really make a go of this?

'See you,' she said, and took her tray and dirty plate back to the rack.

Stephanie had been called in to the maternity floor while Daniel was in the middle of performing a Caesarean section for a mum who'd spent the last day and a half in a back-to-back labour. Although she'd really wanted to have a normal delivery, the baby was starting to get distressed and Iris had explained to her that her labour simply wasn't progressing and it wasn't fair on her or the baby. The patient had discussed it with her husband, then agreed, in tears, to a C-section.

After the delivery, Stephanie was doing the newborn checks. She said quietly to Iris, 'The baby's grunting a bit and the Apgar score's a bit low for my liking. I'd like to take her through to Special Care to help her breathing.'

'Agreed,' Iris said.

Stephanie wrapped the baby up and took her over to the parents, noting that the mum was still in tears. 'You have a gorgeous baby girl here.'

'I can't cuddle her until I've been sewn up, can I?' she asked, looking miserable.

'No, but she can hold your finger while her dad gives her a cuddle,' Stephanie reassured her.

'Is she all right?' the dad asked, looking anxious.

'She'll be fine,' Stephanie said. 'But at the moment she's breathing a little bit fast—it's what we call transient tachypnoea of the newborn or TTN. It only lasts for two or three days and we can make her better, but we do need to take her through to the special care unit, once you've had a cuddle.'

'Why has she got this TTN thing? It is a virus or something?' the mum asked.

'No. While the baby's still inside the womb, her lungs are filled with fluid. If you have a vaginal birth, the fluid is squeezed out as the baby passes through the birth canal. With a C-section, that doesn't happen, so there's still some fluid in the lungs. That makes it harder for the baby to take in oxygen, and she breathes faster to make up for it.'

The mum's eyes widened. 'So it's my fault?'

'No, not at all. And it's quite common, so try not to worry. What we're going to do is put her under an oxygen hood for a couple of hours. It will help her breathe normally, and she won't have any problems afterwards. I promise, there's nothing to worry about.'

'Can we see her?' the dad asked.

'You can see her whenever you like in the unit and you'll be able to cuddle her and feed her,' Stephanie reassured them.

'Though for your comfort I'd prefer you to wait until the spinal block has worn off and you can move your legs again,' Daniel said.

'How long will that take?' the mum asked.

'A couple of hours, so she might even come back to you before you get a chance to go to the ward,' Daniel explained.

'You might notice some little grunting sounds when she breathes and her nostrils might flare a bit. She might look a little bit blue round her mouth, and the skin will suck in between her ribs when she breathes, but these are all symptoms of TTN and they'll go away in a couple of days,' Stephanie said. 'If you've got any worries, the midwives will be around, and I happen to know I'm on the roster for doing the first-day checks on the babies tomorrow, so you can ask me anything you like. Even if you think it's little or a silly question—I'd much rather you asked so I can reassure you that everything's fine, rather than sat there worrying.'

'Thank you.' The mum's lower lip wobbled slightly. 'I wanted to feed her myself.'

'And you can,' Stephanie reassured her. 'You've got a beautiful little girl there, so well done.' She rested her hand on the mum's shoulder. 'You take care, and I'll see you in a little bit.'

She sorted out the baby's admission to the special care unit, and took the baby up after the mum had had a brief cuddle; then she came back down to report that the baby had settled in nicely and they could visit whenever they liked.

Daniel caught up with her in the corridor. 'That was a

really nice explanation you gave of TTN. I like the way you reassured the mum.'

She shrugged. 'It's my job.'

'I guess.' He leaned forward and stole a kiss right there in the corridor.

'Dan!' she exclaimed, scandalised.

'Nobody was looking.' He winked at her. 'See you later.'

Stephanie felt herself flushing, but was smiling all the way back to ward. Especially when she checked her phone after her shift to find a message from Dan.

It seems I have a babysitter for tonight. Fancy going to the movies?

She typed back.

Love to. Tell me where and when. Don't mind what we see.

Great. Leicester Square at 7.30.

Daniel was already waiting outside the cinema when he saw Stephanie walk round the corner into Leicester Square. His heart skipped a beat when he saw her. He'd never expected to feel like this again, but Stephanie drew him.

And then there was the fact that their relationship had moved to the next stage. He'd forgotten how much he liked the closeness of lovemaking—not just the sex side, but holding his lover afterwards, feeling warm and sated and just a little bit blissed out, talking about anything and everything. He'd really missed that. He'd missed going for a walk, just holding hands. He'd missed the sweetness of a shared glance. With Stephanie, he'd rediscovered all of it.

She saw him and lifted her hand in acknowledgement, smiling at him.

He met her with a hug, lifted her off her feet and whirled her round, then kissed her.

'Anyone would think you hadn't seen me for ages,' she teased.

'It feels like it.' Weirdly, that was true. He'd missed her. Something else he hadn't expected.

'Poor baby.' She batted her eyelashes at him, and laughed.

'Did you have time to eat anything before you came out?'

'I grabbed a sandwich. How about you?'

'I ate with Mia,' he said. 'Sorry, I should've said.'

'It's fine. It's totally what I expected you to do, so stop worrying.'

She was so in tune with him. And he didn't feel pressured by her; she'd accepted that Mia was a huge part of his life and didn't expect to come first. 'Is a rom-com OK with you?'

'Very OK. I like most sorts of films—well, as long as they're not super-gory,' she said.

He smiled. 'Noted.'

They held hands all the way through the film and fed each other popcorn, making Daniel feel like a teenager again. He'd forgotten what it felt like just to have fun like this.

'Do you want to come back to my place?' Stephanie asked, half shyly, as they left the cinema.

He stole a kiss. 'Would you mind if I didn't? This baby-sitting was a last-minute thing, and although Lucy brought a pile of marking with her—'

'—it's not fair to take her for granted,' Stephanie finished, surprising him by how much in tune she was with him. She kissed him lightly. 'It's OK. I'm happy just being with you, and tonight was an unexpected bonus.'

'I'm happy, too,' he said softly. 'I never thought I would be again, after I lost Meg.'

She gave him a rueful smile. 'Me neither, after my divorce.'

They shared a glance.

Should he tell her he was falling in love with her? Would she work it out for herself that he'd pretty much just told her that?

And was she telling him the same, or was he over-reading this?

He wasn't quite ready to take that risk. He didn't want to scare her off by telling her straight. Instead, he kissed her again. 'I'm glad you're happy.'

She stroked his face. 'Right now, life's good,' she said softly.

In other words, he thought, don't jinx it by saying it out loud. Well, he could live with that. For now.

'Obviously you missed it last time,' the social worker said.

'It's a new break,' Stephanie countered.

'Oh, come on. How likely is it that he's broken his arm again, the day after the cast came off? Unless the foster-parents let his mother see him without telling us.'

Stephanie didn't usually have a problem dealing with people from other departments and institutions, but this particular woman drove her crazy. Once she'd decided something, she wouldn't allow for any alternatives, and Stephanie hated that. 'That's speculation,' Stephanie said, 'and unfair. And surely Oscar Goldblum's health and comfort come first?'

The social worker just glowered at her.

'If you'll excuse me, I have children to treat,' Stephanie said, icily polite and resisting the temptation to yell at the woman and tell her to do her job fairly. Oscar Goldblum had broken his arm for a second time, and he'd been living with foster-parents rather than with his mother; surely that had to cast doubt on the theory that Della was the cause of the fractures?

But at least she was able to talk to Daniel about it after work.

'Stephanie, don't get me wrong, but maybe you're getting a bit too involved?' he said.

'How do you mean?'

'Don't go defensive on me,' he said gently. 'I'm not making a judgement. But you grew up in care and your childhood was maybe not as happy as it could've been, so my guess is that you don't like to see families broken and children put in care. Look at the way you were about Janine.'

'I know, but I was right about her, wasn't I?'

'Yes, but are you sure you're right about this one? I mean *really* right, not just seeing what you want to see?'

She lifted her chin. It stung that he'd actually raised the question. Just like Joe had always questioned her decisions. 'Daniel, I'm a good doctor.'

'I know you are. All I'm saying is that sometimes we get cases where our judgement isn't quite as good as it could be—look at the way I panicked over Mia.'

'You were absolutely right to panic. She has reactive airways and she needed treatment.'

He spread his hands. 'And I should've been able to work that out for myself instead of thinking of all the serious conditions she could have.'

He really was being unfair to himself, she thought. 'She's your daughter.'

'Exactly. And I'm both parents to her, so I feel doubly bound to get everything right, all the time. It's the same sort of thing with you and your patients.'

She looked at him, hurt. 'Dan, that's not fair.'

He squeezed her hand. 'I'm not saying you're wrong about this, just that maybe you need to keep your mind a bit more open.'

What? She wasn't the narrow-minded one here. That was the social worker.

'Is it possible that everyone missed a break last time round?' he asked.

'No. I've reviewed the X-rays from last time. It was a Colles' fracture. According to the notes, Della said he tripped over and put his hands out to stop himself falling, and you know as well as I do that's exactly how Colles' fractures happen. This new one's further up his forearm, but it would've shown up.'

'So you think the foster-parents might've caused the fracture?' he asked.

She wrinkled her nose. 'It's possible, but how likely is it that firstly a parent and then a foster-parent would batter a child? Oscar would have to be incredibly unlucky. Screening of foster-parents is pretty thorough nowadays so, although it's technically possible, I don't think it's the explanation. I think it's much more likely he has a medical condition.'

'And you've got one in mind?'

She nodded. 'Type one osteogenesis imperfecta would explain why Oscar has a history of breaks. I wouldn't be surprised if baby Charlie comes in with another break in the next four months. If one of their parents has OI, then the children have a fifty per cent chance of inheriting it.'

'Brittle bone? Which parent?'

She grimaced. 'That I don't know yet. Della's a little shorter than average, but that's not enough to prove my theory. We'd need to check her properly—see if she has the blue tints to the whites of her eyes, a history of fractures and poor muscle tone. I want to take another look at

Oscar, too. I can check if his birth weight was a little lower than average and see how his teeth are.'

'Talk to Della about her medical history. And you can send her for a DEXA scan to see about the bone density,' he suggested.

'A DEXA scan will show up any problems with Della, but maybe not in the children because they're so young— a tiny baby and a three-year-old.' She frowned. 'We need a skin-punch biopsy to check collagen synthesis, which can take weeks; and DNA testing on a blood sample can take months.'

He nodded. 'And you're worrying about this.'

'Yes,' she admitted. 'It's not that I think all care places are bad, but if there isn't a good reason to split them up then surely it's better for the family to stay together? I said from the start that I don't think it's abuse, and this new fracture makes me more convinced that I'm right and we need to treat the family for OI. I'm really not bringing my own background into this, Dan.'

'OK, I'll get off your case.' He squeezed her hand. 'If there's anything I can do to help, let me know.'

'Thank you. I appreciate it.'

He kissed her. 'There was something else I wanted to talk to you about.'

'Oh?'

'I was thinking...' He paused. 'Maybe we could take Mia out on Saturday.'

What? He wanted her to go out with him on a *family* basis?

That was where it had all gone wrong with Joe.

'Stephanie?' he prompted when she remained silent.

She took a deep breath. 'Are you sure about...well...?'

'Introducing you to my daughter?' He nodded. 'Don't forget, she's already met you and liked you.'

'As her doctor. This is different.'

'You think I'm rushing it?' he asked. 'We've been seeing each other for a few weeks now. I like you, and I think you like me.'

She did. And it scared her. 'How's Mia going to feel about this? I mean, you bringing someone in to...' There was no point in beating about the bush. 'Her mother's place?' Especially as she herself had no real experience of what it was like to *have* a mother, let alone *be* a mother. Mia was six years old. Vulnerable. Stephanie knew she couldn't afford to make a mess of this.

Daniel cupped her face and kissed her lightly on the lips. 'The accident was four years ago. Mia only remembers Meg from photos and videos. She's not going to give you a hard time over this.'

'Isn't she going to need some time to get used to the idea?' Right at that moment, Stephanie thought she could do with some time, too.

'Maybe. But I think she's ready to meet you.' He paused. 'Or would you rather meet the rest of my family first?'

Now he was getting into *really* scary territory. She couldn't get a single word out in reply.

'I know you haven't told me what happened with your ex and his family. I'm not going to press you,' Daniel said. 'But I'll listen whenever you're ready to talk about it.'

Help. What did she say now?

'What I did pick up,' he continued, 'is that you had a hard time with them. You won't get that with mine.' He kissed her lightly. 'I can tell you that until I'm blue in the face, but the only way you'll believe me is if you see if for yourself. Meet them.'

She swallowed hard. Meet them? No, no and no. 'I'm sorry.' The doubts were there and she couldn't get past them. She bit her lip. 'I wish I could be different.'

'Actually, I quite like you as you are.' He stole another kiss. 'Just think about it, OK?'

'OK.'

There was a glint in his eye. 'We've got forty minutes until I need to go back.'

'Indeed.'

'And I have some great ideas on how to use those forty minutes.' He grinned and scooped her up in his arms. 'Me caveman.'

And she pushed her fears aside and laughed back as he carried her through to her bedroom.

CHAPTER TEN

STEPHANIE THOUGHT ABOUT what Daniel had said all that evening, after he'd left.

And all the way to work.

And every second of her shift, in between seeing patients.

He was asking her to take a huge leap of faith. To trust him. And by asking her to go out with him and Mia, he was showing that same trust in her.

Could she do this?

Could she take the risk of being part of a family?

As if he understood that she needed some space, Daniel didn't suggest meeting for lunch, and he didn't call or text her. Or was he feeling the same way that she was—confused, scared, and wanting to back out?

There was only one way to find out. She called him, that evening.

'Hi. How are you doing?' he asked.

'OK,' she fibbed. 'Um, what you said about taking Mia out.'

That got his interest. 'Yes?'

'If you're sure about it, then yes. I'd like to go with you.'

'How about the Natural History Museum?' he suggested. 'It's her favourite place, and she'll enjoy showing you around.'

Neutral territory. Lots of other people around. No pressure. And she could always do a fake call on her mobile phone and say that she'd been called in, if need be. Which meant that if it all went wrong, she wasn't trapped and nobody would get hurt. 'I'd like that.'

'That's great. We'll meet you outside the entrance at ten on Saturday morning.'

She took a deep breath. 'OK.'

'Don't be scared,' he said softly. 'It's all going to be fine.'

She really hoped he was right.

On Saturday morning, Stephanie caught the train through to South Kensington and came out of the Tube entrance to see the beautiful Victorian building. Daniel and Mia were already there, waiting for her. He raised a hand to greet her and she hurried over to them. He looked gorgeous in a mulberry-coloured sweater and jeans, and Stephanie was glad that she'd dressed casually, too.

She crouched down so she was at a level height with Mia. 'Hello, Mia. Do you remember me?'

The little girl nodded, her brown eyes wide. 'Hello, Dr Scott.'

'You can call me Stephanie, if you like.' She smiled at the little girl. 'Thank you for letting me come to see the dinosaurs with you and your dad. I've never seen them before.'

'There's a big, really scary one,' Mia said, 'but it's all right. I'll hold your hand so you don't have to be afraid.'

Stephanie had to swallow the lump in her throat. Mia clearly had the same warm, generous nature as her father; then again, she already knew that from when the little girl had brought in the cakes for the nursing staff after her night on the ward. 'I'd like that. Very much.'

She was amazed by how big the diplodocus was in the main hall.

'Don't worry,' Mia said, 'it didn't eat people, just leaves, so it wouldn't have eaten you.'

She chatted to the little girl about dinosaurs, surprised at how much Mia knew about them.

'Daddy likes dinosaurs,' Mia confided. 'He reads me stories about dinosaurs, too.'

'That sounds like fun.' She shared a glance with Daniel. He was clearly a brilliant father and Mia seemed incredibly well adjusted, confident and cheerful.

She thoroughly enjoyed going round the museum with Daniel and Mia, exclaiming over the dinosaurs, the skeleton of the big blue whale, and her favourite bit, the fossilised lightning.

So this was what being part of a family could feel like. *Being right where you belonged.*

And it was like a sunny spring day with all the daffodils coming out, after months of grey days full of ice and snow.

Daniel was taking a huge risk, opening his life up to her like this. If it went wrong, the two of them wouldn't be the only ones hurt. She really had to make sure she got it right this time.

They went out for a late lunch after the museum. 'This is my treat, to say thank you for taking me to the museum— no arguments, Dan,' she added, with a warning look.

They found a small family restaurant, a chain that Daniel told her Mia liked. The little girl ordered popcorn chicken, fries and a smoothie; Dan ordered Moroccan chicken and couscous; and Stephanie ordered salad with chicken, mango and prawns.

When their food arrived, Mia glanced at Stephanie's plate. 'That looks really nice.'

'Do you want to try it?' Stephanie asked. Then she realised what she'd done. 'If that's OK with your dad, that is,' she added swiftly. Oh, help. She should've checked with Dan first. She'd put him in an awkward position, and that wasn't fair.

He smiled. 'It's fine—provided I get to try it as well.'

She smiled back. She hadn't done any damage yet, then.

He fed her a taste of his chicken from his fork. It felt incredibly intimate; yet, at the same time, it felt as if this was simply part of a normal family meal out—something she'd never quite felt with Joe.

They went for a walk in the park afterwards, and Mia insisted that Stephanie join her on the slide and the swings. It had been years and years since Stephanie had been to a children's playground; she'd forgotten what fun it could be. And sharing this day with Mia and Daniel felt really, really special.

Finally, Daniel said, 'OK, sweetheart—time to head for home. It's starting to get dark.'

'Are you coming, too, Stephanie?' Mia asked

Stephanie didn't want to overstay her welcome; at the same time, she didn't want to push the little girl away. This was clearly an overture. Should he accept it? She looked at Daniel for guidance, and he gave her a tiny nod.

'I'd like that. Thank you for inviting me, Mia.'

It was the first time she'd been to Daniel's house, but it was pretty much what she'd expected: a small, pretty terraced house. The living room was full of books, as well as a state-of-the-art computer and a box of toys for Mia.

'That's my mummy,' Mia said, taking Stephanie's hand and leading her over to the photographs on the mantelpiece.

The house was obviously filled with memories of the past. Meg Connor had been beautiful, and she'd clearly been very much loved. And, even though Stephanie knew it was selfish and inappropriate, she couldn't help a flood of doubt. How was she going to fit into Daniel and Mia's lives? They were already a very tight unit. So this would be exactly the same as it had been with Joe; she'd be the outsider again, never quite sure of her place in their family and knowing that she wasn't really a part of it.

'And that's my favourite picture of us,' Mia said, pointing to the picture of a dark-haired woman holding a toddler in her arms, with a background of a spectacular blue-flowered bush. 'It's in our garden.'

How could she possibly knock the little girl back?

'She's very pretty,' Stephanie said. 'She looks a lot like you.' Though she could see Daniel in the little girl, too; they both had the same warmth in their smiles.

'Do you look like your mummy?' Mia asked.

The question was totally out of left field, and it was a hard one to answer as Stephanie didn't even have a photograph of her mother. In the end, she fudged it with a smile and said, 'Yes, but sadly I don't have a mummy any more either.'

'Did your mummy die?' Mia asked.

'Yes.' Though she'd lie about how, if she had to. No way would Stephanie let that misery hurt Mia, too.

'So we're the same,' Mia said, 'even though your eyes are green and mine are brown.'

'I guess so.' There was a lump in Stephanie's throat.

'Do you want to play a game?' Mia asked.

Safer ground. Something she'd do with her patients, especially the ones who didn't get visitors. 'I'd love to.'

Daniel brought through two mugs of coffee, plus a mug of hot chocolate for Mia, in time to overhear the last bit. 'Games, hmm?'

'You can play, too, Daddy,' Mia said.

They played Snap until Mia had won for the fifth time. 'Enough for now, I think, sweetheart,' Daniel said gently.

Mia looked at Stephanie. 'Will you stay for tea tonight?' she asked.

It was tempting, but Stephanie didn't push it. 'I can't, sweetheart. I have things I need to do back at my flat.'

'That means laundry. Daddy always does laundry on Saturday nights,' Mia said, rolling her eyes. 'And he says ironing is slavery.'

Stephanie had to hide her smile at the thought of Daniel being enslaved to the ironing board. 'He's right.'

'But we have to look smart at work,' Daniel said. 'It gives the patients more confidence in us.'

Mia shook her head. 'It's your face that does that, Daddy, not your suit. You look kind and clever, so people know they can trust you to make them better.' She looked at Stephanie. 'You, too. I was scared when I went to hospital, even though I was with Daddy and Fred Bear, but you stopped me being scared and I knew you'd make me better.'

Stephanie felt the tears filming her eyes. 'I'm glad.'

'Out of the mouths of babes,' Daniel said when he saw Stephanie to the door. 'She's right. You're kind and you're clever.' He paused. 'And you make the world feel a better place.'

She felt the same way about him. And the hope in her heart burned just that little bit brighter.

Daniel called Stephanie later that night. 'You were a huge hit with Mia.'

'I'm glad.'

'Not that I want to put you under any pressure, you understand, but before she went to sleep she gave me strict instructions to call you and ask if you'll come to the aquarium with us next weekend.'

'She really wants me to come?' He wasn't just saying that?

'She really wants you to come,' he confirmed. 'And so do I.' He paused. 'That is…if you want to see us again. I worried that maybe it put you off when you saw the photos of Meg. You wouldn't stay for tea.'

'I didn't want to overstay my welcome,' she said lightly. 'Dan, of course you're going to have pictures of Mia's mum around. I wouldn't expect anything else.'

'Just as long as you know it doesn't mean…' He sighed. 'We should be having this conversation face to face.'

'It's OK.' But his words intrigued her, at the same time as they worried her. 'What were you going to say?'

'It's been four years. Of course I still miss Meg. And she'll always be part of my life. But I'm at the point now where I'm ready to move on.' He sighed again. 'Which isn't meant to put pressure on you.'

'Do you really think I'm that fragile?'

'No.' But he didn't sound too sure.

'Dan?'

'Not fragile, no. But I think you had a hard time growing up, and you're clearly not used to a family situation. Whatever happened with your ex, I think it's made you wary. And it's a lot to ask, expecting someone to take me on as a package.'

'I met Mia at the same time as I met you, remember,' she said softly. 'And she's a lovely little girl. You're doing a fantastic job of bringing her up to be as warm and kind as you are.'

'I wasn't fishing for compliments,' he said.

'I know. And I didn't say it because I thought you were,' she said.

'Are you ready to move on?' he asked softly. 'To think about taking this forward?'

'Do you mean, meet the rest of your family?'

He laughed. 'Not yet. I know that's a big ask.' He

paused. 'But, yes, I'd like you to meet them in the future. Just take this day by day for now, hmm?'

Day by day. Give her time to get used to the idea. 'That works for me.'

The following weekend, Stephanie and Daniel took Mia to the aquarium. The little girl held Stephanie's hand and pointed out her favourite fish. And on the Sunday, Stephanie cooked them a roast dinner at her flat, with strawberries and ice cream for pudding.

'You're a better cook than Daddy,' Mia said with a smile. 'Daddy tries. But he's better at breaded chicken and oven chips.'

Stephanie smiled. 'Well, I like cooking.' She'd taught herself and made plenty of mistakes, but now she was happy to try new recipes and even tinker with them before she tried cooking them.

'Is that your sister?' Mia asked, looking at the photographs on the fridge.

'No, my best friend, Trish. And that's her little boy, Calum—he's my godson.'

'So you're sort of a mummy, then,' Mia said thoughtfully.

'Sort of. I like children.' In her experience they didn't judge you the way adults did. They took you for who you were rather than who they wanted you to be.

'I like you,' Mia said solemnly.

Stephanie hugged her. 'Good. Because I like you, too.'

Though when Mia gave her a small parcel wrapped in tissue paper, the next weekend, there was a real lump in her throat when she opened it. It was a home-made picture frame, with pasta shapes glued onto a cardboard frame and then spray-painted silver, and in the middle of the frame was a photograph someone had taken for them at the aquarium: the three of them together, with Mia in the middle.

'I made it with Aunty Lucy, after school,' Mia said solemnly. 'She helped me a bit with the paint, but I did the rest of it.'

'It's beautiful,' Stephanie said. 'Thank you very, very much. And I'm going to put it right here on the mantelpiece, where everyone can see it.'

Mia beamed, looking pleased. 'You really like it?'

'I really, *really* like it,' Stephanie said, hugging her.

So maybe this was going to work out. Mia had seemed to accept her, and she was growing closer to Daniel. The only sticking point now would be if his family didn't like her—and if Meg's parents couldn't cope with the idea of someone else in their daughter's place. She knew she'd have to face it eventually, but for now she was happy in their little bubble—just the three of them.

CHAPTER ELEVEN

STEPHANIE CHECKED HER diary for the sixth time. And she reached the same horrible conclusion for the sixth time too: her period was late.

And, thanks to the Pill, her period was *never* late. She was regular down to the hour of the day. Maybe the stress of the Goldblum case was making her period go haywire, she thought. Then again, she was on the Pill to regulate her periods, so stress shouldn't make a difference. She shouldn't miss a period, ever.

Then she went cold.

Could she actually be pregnant?

She and Daniel had had that takeaway meal a couple of weeks ago, and they'd both had an upset stomach the following day. So, technically, it was possible that she could be pregnant. The upset stomach could mean that the Pill hadn't worked, and she remembered that they'd made love that night, after the meal. Before she'd been ill. Sperm could live for five days inside her body. So if she'd been ovulating that day...

No, no and *no*.

The risks of actually conceiving were tiny.

She couldn't be pregnant.

It would be a total disaster. Just as it had been when

she'd last fallen pregnant—when she'd tried to be a surrogate mother and carry a baby for Joe's sister.

And why did this have to happen the same week as the anniversary of her miscarriage?

She'd have to take a pregnancy test. But her period was only *just* late. It might be too soon for the HGC hormone to show up, so the test could give a false negative. She'd give it a few days—a week—and see if her period started.

In the meantime, she avoided Daniel, not wanting to burden him with her worries. Maybe she was being a coward; but on the other hand there was Trish's favourite saying about not troubling trouble. Until she knew for definite that there was a problem, what was the point of telling him and worrying him, too?

But she didn't tell Trish, either. She knew her best friend would worry about her and rush straight down to London to see her, and she also knew that Trish had enough worries of her own; Trish's husband's job was under threat of redundancy. So it was better to keep this to herself until she knew what was going on.

At least it was half term, so Daniel was taking time off to be with Mia and she didn't have to see him at work. She was guiltily aware that they'd made plans for her to take leave, too—but she couldn't do that, not when all this was up in the air.

The fib was easy, especially as she did it by text:

Sorry, short of staff, bug going round, they need me in at work.

But she felt even guiltier when Daniel called her and was nice about it. 'You must be up to your eyes if people are off sick. Come over to ours for dinner after work—then you won't have to cook.'

'Sorry, Dan. I'm doing split shifts.' Another lie.

'OK. Though Mia says to tell you she misses you.'

Oh, help. She missed Mia, too. And Dan. This wasn't fair. 'Tell her I'm sorry. And I'll make it up to her.' If she had the chance.

'I will, but the offer's open. You don't have to give us notice—just turn up.'

She really, *really* didn't deserve this. And her voice cracked when she whispered, 'Thank you.'

Somehow she managed to get through the next couple of days, keeping her distance and lying through her teeth. But then Daniel sent her a text.

Being a guy, I can bit a bit slow on the uptake sometimes. Have I done something to upset you?

Guilt flooded through her as she read the words.

If I have, then I apologise—and please let me know what I've done so I can make sure I don't do it again.

Oh, help. How mean was she, just staying out of his way and not telling him what was wrong, especially as none of this was his fault? She wasn't being fair.

But she also couldn't tell him what was wrong. Not until she knew for certain.

In the meantime, what did she say to him?

This really wasn't his fault. Daniel hadn't done anything to upset her. But she wasn't ready to have a conversation about babies and families. It would change everything. How would he feel about the idea of having more children? Even if he wanted more children, surely Mia would need time to get used to the idea too. Yes, she was bonding with the little girl, but all of this was happening way too fast. They needed time.

And Stephanie definitely wasn't ready to move on to the next stage. To go public. Be an item with him. It scared her rigid; that was when everything had started to go wrong between herself and Joe. Both of them had been too stubborn to heed the warnings when his family hadn't taken to her. She wouldn't make that mistake again.

What a mess. She typed back.

It's not you

But that sounded like the beginning of a Dear John letter, as if she was planning to dump him. Which she wasn't. She was just waiting until she knew what was happening.

She deleted the words, and instead typed in:

Just got a lot on my plate right now.

That was true enough, though she was guiltily aware that she was skirting the issue. But she couldn't see him yet. Not until she knew whether she was pregnant or not. She just couldn't. It wouldn't be fair to either of them. Not that the current situation was fair, either; but right now she felt as if she was caught between a rock and a hard place.

On the Tuesday evening, Stephanie caught the Tube to the West End on the way home from work, called into a pharmacy where she knew she'd be totally anonymous, and bought a pregnancy test from a shelf festooned with tinsel and Christmas decorations. Ha. This could turn out to be her very worst Christmas yet, and she'd already had quite a few tough ones in her thirty years.

She felt sick, but hopefully that was owing to adrenalin and worry rather than pregnancy hormones. This wasn't like the last time she'd taken a pregnancy test. Unless she was totally in denial. God, if only Daniel was here. But that was selfish. She couldn't burden him with her miseries. He had enough to deal with.

Her steps dragged as she walked back from the Tube station to her flat. Once she'd closed the front door behind her, she closed her eyes and leaned back against it. 'Get a grip,' she told herself fiercely. 'You need to know the truth so you can work out what to do next.' If the test was negative, maybe she could pretend that the last few days hadn't happened and try to rescue her relationship with Daniel. And if it was positive...

Well, she'd cross that bridge when she came to it.

She took a deep breath and headed for the bathroom. Even though she knew that the digital pregnancy tests gave reasonably quick results, it still felt as though it took for ever for the two minutes to tick round. Two minutes in which she restored order to her clothes, washed her hands and tidied the bathroom—even though it didn't actually need tidying.

And then the two minutes were up.

Crunch time.

Pregnant, or not pregnant?

Her hand was shaking and her mouth was dry as she lifted the stick to look at the test window. This one tiny little result could change her entire life.

Not pregnant.

Relief made her knees buckle and she had to hold on to the sink.

She wasn't pregnant. Life wasn't going to change. She and Daniel could still carry on exactly as they were. Everything was fine.

Though, at the same time, it wasn't fine at all. Because all the memories slammed into her. Memories of doing a pregnancy test before, of her hand shaking and her mouth being dry, because it was so, so important that the test should be positive. Memories of the relief in Joe's face when she told him that the procedure had worked. Memories of the joy in Kitty's face when they'd told her the news—that the implantation had been successful and Kitty was finally going to have the baby she'd wanted to desperately.

And memories of the choking disappointment, only a few weeks later, when she'd lost the baby. Seeing Kitty's dreams shatter. Seeing the joy in her face turn to hatred.

It took Stephanie a while to realise that her face was wet.

And a while longer to realise that her doorbell was buzzing.

Hopefully whoever it was would just go away.

Except they didn't. They just kept ringing her doorbell, as if they knew she was there and they weren't going to give up until she answered.

She gave in and made her way to the hallway. She picked up the entryphone with a shaking hand and just hoped that her emotion didn't show in her voice. 'Yes?'

'Stephanie?'

Oh, no. Of all the people she didn't want to face right now. 'Daniel.'

'Can I come up?'

Her brain had temporarily gone into frozen mode and she couldn't think of an excuse. 'I…'

'Stephanie?'

If she said no, she knew he'd push her for an explanation. 'OK.'

She didn't have time to splash her face with water; she could only hope that her eyes weren't too red and puffy.

Though the first thing he did when he walked in— after handing her some gorgeous flowers that she didn't deserve—was to put his hands on her shoulders and look at her. 'You look as if you've been crying.'

She could hardly deny it. 'I, um… Yeah.'

'What's wrong?'

'That's a bit of a difficult question, and there isn't a short answer,' she said. 'I need to put these beautiful flowers in water. Can I make you a mug of tea?'

It was obvious from the expression on his face that he knew she was trying to sidestep the issue and buy herself some time, but to her relief he let her get away with it. 'That'd be nice.'

He waited until she'd put both mugs of tea on the kitchen table before wrapping his arms round her. 'Talk to me.'

She owed it to him. She knew that. So why couldn't she get the words out? She simply stared at him, wide-eyed, wishing she knew what to say.

'OK. Let's try it another way. Why have you been avoiding me?'

'Because…' She had to be honest. 'I was scared it was all going to go wrong between us.'

'Why would it go wrong between us?'

That was the big question. And she didn't have a clue how he was going to react when she told him.

'Stephanie?'

She blew out a breath. 'There isn't an easy way to say this.'

'Then tell me straight.'

'Because I thought I might be pregnant.'

He went very, very still. 'And are you?'

She couldn't tell a thing from his voice. It was totally inscrutable. Was he shocked, angry, hurt? She didn't have a clue. 'No-o.' And her voice *would* have to waver.

'Is that why you were crying?'

She gulped. Another tough question, but she owed him the truth. 'Yes.'

'Because you were relieved?' He paused. 'Or because you were disappointed?'

A messed-up mixture of the two. 'It's complicated.' She pulled away. 'Let's sit down.' Hopefully it would be easier to talk to him with the table between them. A little bit of distance.

He waited. Patiently. And she cracked.

'I've been here before,' she whispered.

'Is that why your marriage broke up? Because you were pregnant?'

She shook her head. 'Because I lost the baby. And, I guess, worrying that maybe I was pregnant because we'd both been ill after that prawn thing and maybe that meant the Pill hadn't worked…it brought everything back to me. Everything that happened. And that probably makes me the wettest person in the world, to cry over something that happened a long time ago.'

'I'm not judging you,' Daniel said.

'No, but you were honest with me about your past. I haven't told you much at all about mine.' She should've told him about this weeks ago. She sighed. 'Joe and I met at a party, in my third year as a student. I was twenty-one; he was five years older than me, worked in banking. I fell in love with him, and when he asked me to marry him I said yes. I thought we'd be fine together, both of us professionals looking for a good career. I thought I'd be part of a family.' The family she'd wanted so very much.

Daniel said nothing; he simply waited while she stared into her mug of tea.

In the end, she broke the silence. 'But his family never really took to me. I think it was from my being brought up in care—they were always just that little bit suspicious of me. They never asked, but I knew they were thinking it. What was so wrong with me, that my parents had obviously given me up and nobody wanted to adopt me? Why was I so unlovable?'

He still said nothing, but he reached across the table to squeeze her hand, and kept his hand folded round hers.

'I never really felt part of Joe's family. I never knew what to say to them. Maybe they thought I was being snotty with them because I was a bit quiet around them.' She shrugged. 'I wasn't being snotty. I'm just not used to families and I'm not very good with them.'

'You're good with Mia,' he said.

'That's different.'

'How?'

'It just is.'

'And you're good with people,' he said softly. 'I've seen you with patients and staff.'

'Because it's my job. And I work in an institution. I can do institutions. I understand how they work. But families? They're so much more complicated. I don't get the dynamics.' She'd never really explained that to anyone before, not even Trish. 'I don't get how siblings feel about each other, because I've never had one. I don't understand the rivalry, or the blood-is-thicker-than-water stuff, or anything like that.' She blew out a breath. 'I did make an effort, really I did. Joe's older sister, Kitty—she was desperate for a baby. She tried and tried and tried to conceive, but she couldn't. She had PCOS.'

'That's tough.'

Being an obstetrician, Daniel would know all about polycystic ovary syndrome, Stephanie knew. 'She was thirty-five. Time was running out for her. She tried fertility drugs, she tried laparascopic ovarian drilling to stop her ovaries producing testosterone, she tried insulin-sensitising drugs in the hope they'd kick-start the fertility drugs into working, but nothing worked. Nothing at all. And every month she was getting more and more desperate for a baby, more and more depressed.' She closed her eyes.

'And then Kitty said they were thinking about asking a surrogate mum to carry a baby for her. An IVF baby, so it would be her egg and Robin's sperm—meaning it would still be their biological baby, even though she couldn't carry it herself. And I thought…I thought maybe this was something I could do for her. That maybe it would bring us closer. That maybe it would help her—and the rest of the family—accept me as Joe's partner.'

'You already had a child?' Daniel asked.

She shook her head. 'I know that's usually one of the criteria, but in special circumstances that's relaxed. Joe and I talked about it. Really talked. We went through all the implications—well, nearly all. I didn't admit that I was doing it because I wanted his family to like me, probably because I knew it was completely the wrong reason and I was being selfish. I said I could see what not being able to have a baby was doing to Kitty and I wanted to do something to help.

'And that was true, Dan. I *did* want to help. Joe and I weren't quite ready to have our own family—I was twenty-five, just qualified, so I wanted to wait for a bit—but we could do this for Kitty and Robin without our lives being radically changed. Joe was happy for me to do it—he'd seen how being childless was destroying his sister. And so we went ahead with the surrogacy.'

She swallowed hard. 'Kitty was so grateful. She was there when I went to book in with the midwife, and she came to the dating scan. She cried when she saw the baby on the screen. And what I'd hoped for? It happened, Dan. Joe's family finally started to accept me. Kitty and I even started to be friends. I know maybe it was the wrong reason to do it, that I was thinking of myself more than her, but I wanted so much to be part of their family.'

'No, I can understand that,' he said softly.

She sighed. 'And then I broke their hearts. I lost the baby.'

'You had a miscarriage?'

She nodded. 'At twelve weeks. The day before Kitty was going to tell everyone that she and Robin were going to be parents. And it was my fault.'

Daniel frowned. 'How do you work that out?'

She grimaced. 'If I hadn't been on duty…'

He shook his head. 'That's not fair. Plenty of pregnant women work and manage to carry a baby to term. It wasn't your fault, Stephanie, and it wasn't because you were working.'

'Once the pregnancy was confirmed, Kitty and Robin wanted me to take a sabbatical until after the baby was born. I said no. I didn't want to give up my job. I love being a paediatrician. Maybe if I hadn't been so selfish about it, the pregnancy would've gone to full term.'

'And maybe it wouldn't. Babies and pregnancy are *my* specialty, remember,' he said gently. 'There are plenty of reasons why women miscarry. One in five pregnancies end up with a miscarriage, and most of them happen before thirteen weeks. Did your obstetrician say why you lost the baby—if there were any issues with hormone levels or if you had any blood clotting disorder?'

'No.'

'Most miscarriages happen because of chance abnormalities in the foetus,' he said. 'It wasn't your fault. It wasn't anything you did or didn't do.'

'No? I'd had some spotting the previous day. I should've

taken notice of that and called in sick, instead of ignoring it and working my shift.'

'Plenty of women experience spotting in the first trimester. Was the bleeding heavy or painful?'

'Well—no,' she admitted.

'Then it wasn't anything to worry about.'

'I miscarried at work, the next day,' she said softly. 'So, actually, I think it *was* something to worry about.'

'The miscarriage still wasn't something you could have prevented, honey.' He moved round to her side of the table, scooped her up and settled her on his lap so he could hold her close. 'That's with my professional hat on. I'm being honest with you, not trying to make you feel better. Surely your obstetrician told you that?'

She swallowed hard. 'It wasn't my baby. It wasn't my place to grieve.'

He stroked her hair. 'Yes, it was, just as much as if the egg had been yours and you weren't the surrogate. You were the one carrying the baby. Of course you were going to grieve when you miscarried. It'd be upsetting for anyone.'

'Kitty was in bits. I destroyed her dreams, Dan. She couldn't forgive me for that. Ever.'

'Maybe at first she blamed you because she was grieving, Stephanie, and it was easier to lash out at you than accept that you'd lost the baby. But she must've realised that you couldn't have done anything to prevent it.'

Stephanie shook her head. 'She couldn't forgive me, and neither could Joe.'

He stared at her, looking shocked. 'Your husband blamed you, too?'

She gave him a sad smile. 'That's what I was saying about blood being thicker than water. And wouldn't you support your sister?'

'If she was in the right, of course I would. And, if she wasn't, then I'd try to talk her round to a more reasonable point of view. Because I love Lucy and I wouldn't want her to get things so badly wrong and end up in a needless mess when it could all be sorted out.' He blew out a breath. 'I'm sorry you had to go through something as painful as that.'

She shrugged. 'I did tell you I wasn't any good at families.'

'Honey, believe me, that really isn't what a family's about. Families pull together. They support each other.'

'Only if you're really one of them,' she said. And she hadn't been. At all.

'It sounds as if they were all upset and you were the easy scapegoat. It wasn't fair of them to blame you—and it's definitely not fair of you to blame yourself. Especially as you're a qualified doctor and you already know all the stuff I just quoted at you.' He stroked her hair and gave her the sweetest, sweetest smile that made her want to bawl all over him. 'I guess it's my turn to teach you to suck eggs.'

'I guess.'

'You do know it wasn't your fault, don't you?'

She grimaced. 'There's a bit of a difference between knowing something with your head and knowing it with your heart, Dan. I went over and over everything I'd done for the previous few weeks, trying to work out if there was anything I'd done to cause the miscarriage.'

'And you found nothing.'

'Maybe if I'd taken it easier…'

'It would still have happened.' He held her close. 'When did it happen?'

'Four years ago this week,' she admitted.

He stroked her hair. 'Oh, Stephanie. So this has brought back all the bad memories for you.' He looked sad. 'I wish you'd told me.'

She shook her head. 'You already have enough on your plate. I wasn't going to dump that on you.'

He kissed her lightly. 'I still have space for you.'

She felt the tears prick her eyelids again. Why did he have to be so nice about everything? Why couldn't he be a control freak like Joe—the control freak she'd thought he was at work? Then it would be so much easier to walk away.

She didn't trust herself to speak and she didn't know what to say anyway, so she stayed silent.

'So that's why you split up with Joe?' Daniel asked.

She nodded. 'I could see it in his face every time he looked at me. The blame. The guilt. It got to the point where I hated going home at night.' The little terraced house she'd done up with Joe, where they'd loved and laughed and been so happy at first, hadn't felt like home to her from the minute she'd driven herself home from the hospital after the miscarriage. She'd felt like an interloper. Unwanted. Despised.

'In the end, I gave up and left, the week before Christmas. I didn't take anything with me except my clothes. My best friend put me up for a couple of nights until I managed to find myself a flat.'

'I can't believe he'd just let you go like that. Surely he realised how upset you were?'

'But I wasn't the one who'd lost her dreams. He couldn't forgive me for making a promise to his sister and not keeping it.'

'Through no fault of your own.'

'I still didn't keep my promise. I didn't have the baby for her.'

'What about his promises to you? You were married.'

'Between the guilt and the blame and the resentment, there wasn't anything left of our marriage worth fighting for. I think we both knew that. The divorce went through on the grounds of irreconcilable differences.' She gave him a sad little smile.

'He hasn't been in touch with you since?'

'Only through his lawyer. And neither of us went to court for the hearing. We both knew it was the end of the road for us. There was no point in heaping up bitterness on top of bitterness. I didn't want anything from him.' Only what he hadn't been able to give her. A stable family, one that loved her for herself.

'I'm sorry you had to go through all that. No wonder you were wary of relationships afterwards—anyone would be, in your shoes.'

'You went through a tougher time. You lost your wife and you had to deal with your daughter's grief as well as your own,' she pointed out.

'Yes, but I had people to support me. It sounds as if you were totally alone.'

'Not totally. I had Trish. My best friend. She's the family I'd choose to have.'

'I'm glad she was there for you.' He stroked her face. 'Why didn't you talk to me before? When you first thought you might be pregnant?'

'Because I panicked.'

'Did you think I'd walk away from you?'

'No. But I worried that you'd feel trapped. And this is all too soon. What about Mia? She's just getting to know me. It's…it's a mess.' She sighed. 'Like I said, I'm not good at family stuff. I had no idea how you'd react.' She didn't dare look at him, too scared to see the answers in his face; but she needed to know the truth. She had to ask the question. 'What if I had been pregnant?'

CHAPTER TWELVE

'THEN WE WOULD'VE worked something out. Talked about what we both wanted.'

This was getting seriously scary, Stephanie thought. As if they were talking about more than just a fling. As if they were talking about having a real relationship. As if they were talking about a *future*.

'What do you want, Stephanie?' he asked.

You. Mia. A family.

And no way could she admit that. Especially as she didn't know exactly how Daniel felt. He might have given her signals, but she knew she was rubbish at interpreting them. Work was fine; friendship, she could do; but relationships were like walking through a room with a blindfold and headphones on, so she couldn't help tripping over every obstacle instead of avoiding them. 'I don't know,' she mumbled.

Gently, he cupped her face in his hands and moved her so she had to look at him. 'Are you going to ask me what I want?'

And now he was moving her really outside her comfort zone. She didn't want to ask. She was too scared about what the answer might be.

'Ask me,' he said softly.

What choice did she have? Her pulse rate spiking, she asked, 'What do you want?'

'You,' he said softly. 'I want *you*, Stephanie. And I don't mean just having sex with you, much as I like that. I mean I want to be with you.'

She felt her eyes widen. He wanted her. Which meant taking things more seriously. 'You mean you want to move our relationship on to the next stage?'

He nodded.

Exactly what he'd suggested a few weeks ago. 'You want me to meet—' her mouth felt as if it was full of sand '—your family.'

'Yes. They're not like Joe's family. They won't judge you and find you wanting.'

'How do you know? I'm rubbish at families. I don't fit in.' She dragged in a breath. 'And how am I ever going to measure up to Meg? She was perfect.'

'No, Meg wasn't perfect,' he corrected. 'She was human. We had our fights, just like every other couple. I loved her deeply, and there will always be a part of my heart that belongs to her,' he said. 'But love isn't like a pie, Stephanie. You don't slice it up and suddenly there isn't anything left. It grows and changes with you.'

That wasn't her experience. At all. So how could she believe him?

'Stephanie, I'm not asking you to step into Meg's place,' he said gently. 'I don't want you as a substitute. I want you for *you*. I'm asking you to step into your own place in my family.'

Her own place. As part of his family. Was it really going to be that easy?

And did he really know his family that well? Joe had thought that his family would accept her, and they hadn't. What was to say that Daniel's family would be any different? Mia seemed to like her, but what if Stephanie was misreading the signals?

'I need to be honest with you.' It was the least he deserved. 'This absolutely terrifies me,' she said.

'Don't overthink it,' he said softly, and stole a kiss. 'I know what I'm asking scares you. Now you've told me what happened with your ex, I understand why. But this is different, and I'll be beside you every step of the way.'

Joe had made a similar promise. And he'd broken it. Even if Daniel meant well—and Stephanie was sure he did—how could he be so sure that he could keep his promise? How could he know that circumstances wouldn't change? And what if his family really didn't like her? She couldn't ask him to choose between them. She'd just have to back off. She'd lose, just as she'd lost last time.

'Mia likes you,' he said. 'Just in case you were worrying about that.'

She swallowed hard. 'But what you're talking about is different. It means being a mum to her.'

'She told me she wanted a mum,' he said softly.

Was that why he was dating her? Because he was looking for a mother for his daughter, not because he really wanted her? The questions must have shown on her face, because he said, 'That isn't why I asked you out.'

'So why *did* you ask me out?' She needed this spelled out. Preferably in words of one syllable.

'Because you drew me,' he said simply. 'You're the first woman I've actually noticed as a woman in four years. The first woman I've wanted to be with.'

And she wanted to be with him, too. But she couldn't get past the fear.

'I need to think about it,' she said again.

And it would be a lot easier to think straight if he wasn't holding her.

As if he guessed what she was thinking, he stroked her face. 'OK. I'll give you some space. As long as you promise to talk to me when you've worked out what you want. I mean *really* talk.'

She nodded. 'I promise.'

'So we'll talk about this again in, say, a week? Next Thursday night?'

She knew she couldn't make him wait indefinitely. And he was being more than patient with her. Given that this couldn't be easy for him either—he had Mia to worry about, too—the least she could do was agree. 'That's fair. A week.' Surely she'd manage to get her head together by then? 'We'll talk then.'

'OK.'

She slid off his lap, not trusting herself not to give in to the urge to ask him to stay with her, and he clearly took it as a sign that she wanted him to leave right now, because he pushed his chair back.

'I'll stay out of your way for now,' he said.

'I'm sorry, Dan. I wish I could be different,' she said. She wished she could stop herself being scared and let herself trust him. But she'd been there before and she'd had a hard time picking up the pieces when it had all gone wrong. She wasn't sure she could do it a second time.

'Don't apologise.' He brushed his mouth against hers in the sweetest, sweetest kiss, and she had a job to hold the tears back.

'Until next week,' he said. 'I'll see myself out.'

Just as he'd promised, he kept his distance over the next couple of days. It was what she'd asked for, so why did it feel so bad? Why was she missing him like crazy and worrying that, now he was giving her space, he'd change his mind about her?

* * *

'Daddy, when are we going out with Stephanie again?' Mia asked.

'Soon, darling.' He hoped. And it was so hard, giving Stephanie the space she'd asked for when all he wanted to do was to hold her close and make her realise how he felt about her.

'Aren't you friends any more?'

Out of the mouths of babes. Help. He'd tried to keep his worries away from Mia, but she'd clearly picked up that something was wrong. 'She's really busy at work right now,' he prevaricated. 'Like when I have to go in to make someone better and Nanna Parker or Nanna Connor comes to look after you.'

'Sometimes,' Mia said, her little face serious, 'I fall out with Ashley at school.' Her best friend, Daniel knew. 'And then we make up and we're friends again.'

Was his daughter giving him relationship advice?

He was torn between amusement and being deeply touched that she cared so much. And they were very wise words from all of her six years. He hugged her. 'I love you, Mia,' he said.

'I love you too, Daddy.' She hugged him back. 'If you fell out with Stephanie, say sorry. She'll say sorry, too, just like me and Ashley do. And then you can be friends again and we can go to Nanna Connor's firework party together.'

The party his parents held every year. So Stephanie would be meeting his whole family at once; he knew that would be a huge ask. 'We'll see, darling. She might have to work,' he said.

But when Mia was in bed that evening, the guilt kicked in. He had no idea whether Stephanie would give his family a chance, or if it would be too much for her—if her experience with Joe's family had damaged her too much to allow her to trust again. And, if she walked away, Mia would be so hurt. He sighed. He'd been an idiot. Rushed everything. He'd pushed Stephanie into meeting Mia before she was really ready, and now—thanks to his selfishness—his daughter could end up badly hurt.

Had he expected too much, thinking that Stephanie could fit into their lives? Thinking that she could put her past behind her and reach out to a future with him and Mia?

Maybe he should let her off the hook and call the whole thing off. Maybe that would be the fairest thing for all of them.

On Monday morning, Stephanie was on duty in the paediatric assessment unit. She was walking into the reception of the emergency department to call the next patient on her list when paramedics rushed past her with a trolley. She recognised the woman on the trolley as Della Goldblum.

What on earth had happened?

Marina Fenton came to meet the paramedics for the handover, and Stephanie heard the words 'beaten up' as they went down the corridor. Someone had punched Della? She thought of Della's partner, who was in prison for GBH. Had he been let out and discovered that the children were in care, blamed Della for it and then started using his fists to ask the questions?

Not that now was the right time to ask. Della wasn't her patient; the children were. Even so, Stephanie was concerned. At the end of her shift, she went into the emergency department reception and asked quietly about Della.

'Are you treating her, Dr Scott?' the receptionist asked.

It was a reminder that this definitely wasn't her place, but she bluffed it out. 'I'm treating her children, and I wanted a quick word with her about it. Has she been discharged, do you know?'

The receptionist looked up the record on the computer. 'She's been admitted to the general surgical ward.'

'Right. I'll go and see if they'd mind me having a quick chat. Thanks for your help,' Stephanie said.

She knew the surgical ward had a strict no-flowers policy, or she could've taken Della something to cheer her up. As it was, she had to go empty-handed.

'Dr Scott.' Della looked bruised and tired; she was on a drip.

'What happened to you?' Stephanie asked softly.

'I ran into some of the neighbours.'

Stephanie felt her eyes widen. 'Your neighbours did this to you?'

'They heard the kids had been taken into care, about the fractures.' Della swallowed hard. 'They decided I was obviously a child-batterer and needed to be taught a lesson.'

Stephanie stared at her, shocked. Without any proof, the neighbours had delivered some rough justice. Mob justice. 'Della, that's so…' She shook her head. 'I really don't know what to say.'

'The doctor says I'm going to be in here for a while. I've got broken ribs. She said something about flail chest.'

Work, not emotional stuff. Stephanie could deal with that. 'It means there's more than one break in at least two of your ribs, so the bone can move freely,' she explained. 'It affects the way your lungs expand when you breathe.'

'It hurts to breathe,' Della said. 'They've given me an epidural—like when I had the kids.' A tear trickled down her cheek. 'I miss them so much.'

'What did the doctor say?'

Della grimaced. 'I can't talk to him. They gave me an X-ray and he says I've got healed rib fractures. He decided it's because someone must've hit me hard enough to break my ribs at some time in the past, and because I've been battered that makes me more likely to hit my kids.'

Someone who'd been abused often turned into an abuser. Stephanie knew the theory.

Della dragged in a breath. 'But I've never hit them, never. And nobody's ever hit me until the neighbours jumped me in the corridor, and I've never had broken ribs. I'd know if I had broken bones, wouldn't I?'

Unless she had osteogenesis imperfecta. Brittle bones. In which case her tolerance for pain was much higher than the average person's. And in which case she must be in major pain right now, to need an epidural.

'I know my bloke's doing time for GBH, but he's never violent with me. He just lost it with the other guy. He knows he shouldn't have done it, and he's having anger management therapy while he's in prison.'

Stephanie felt guilty about the fact she'd jumped to a similar conclusion about Della's partner without knowing the facts. It made her almost as bad as the people who'd beaten Della up. 'Mmm,' she said noncommittally.

'I'll never, ever get my children back now, and I love them so much. I hate it that they're going to grow up without me. It's so wrong.'

She sat holding Della's hand while the woman sobbed, feeling helpless.

My mother must've been through something like this, she thought, lonely and desperate when I was taken away from me instead of being given the support she needed. Would Della end up making the same mistake and take her own life?

'Della, try not to cry like this. It's going to make your ribs hurt even more,' she said gently.

'I don't care,' Della sobbed. 'I don't care about anything any more. Not without my kids.'

How could she just stand aside and let that happen? 'I'll go and see if I can have a word with your doctor. Try not to worry. We'll sort something out.'

She went to find the doctor on duty, and glanced at his hospital identity badge.

'Can I have a quick word about one of your patients, please, Dr Hamilton?' she asked.

He frowned. 'Are you a relative?'

'No. I'm Stephanie Scott from the children's ward. I'm treating the children of one of your patients, and I think their cases might be relevant to her injuries. Della Goldblum.'

Dr Hamilton looked thoughtful. 'The woman who was beaten up.'

'And who *isn't* a baby-batterer,' Stephanie said firmly. 'Though her children have both been in with fractures.'

'So they're clumsy, hmm?' Dr Hamilton asked, sounding unconvinced.

'Can we go somewhere a bit more private to talk?' she asked.

For a moment, she thought he was going to refuse. Then he nodded and led her into an office. 'OK. So what's this about?'

'I know Della was beaten up, but the fact she's got so many fractures—it's not necessarily because of the force they used. And there are a few old fractures on her X-rays.'

'From past beatings,' Dr Hamilton said.

'She says not. And she can't remember ever breaking any bones. I don't think she's in denial—I think she's got a high tolerance for pain.'

Dr Hamilton frowned. 'This sounds as if you have a theory.'

Stephanie nodded. 'I think she has osteogenesis imperfecta. Daniel Connor in Maternity thinks it's a possibility, too. I did book a skin biopsy for the children to test the collagen, but as you know it takes at least six weeks to culture the cells. The results aren't back yet.'

'Did you order DNA tests?' Dr Hamilton asked.

Stephanie shook her head. 'They take at least three months, and I didn't think it would be that helpful. What I'm thinking is a DEXA scan—though obviously I couldn't order that on her because she's not my patient.' But Dr Hamilton could order it.

'OI. Hmm.' He glanced at his watch. 'It's too late to send her down to X-Ray now. But what you've just said makes a lot of sense to me. We'll get a DEXA scan done on Della tomorrow to check her bone density. If it *is* suspected OI, then we need to start physio and get her mobile as quickly as possible, because prolonged immobilisation can weaken the bones further and cause muscle loss.' He frowned. 'It worries me now that she's got an epidural so she can't move. I'll have to talk to her about different forms of pain relief. Obviously I can't leave her in pain, but if she has OI then we need to keep her mobile.'

Stephanie had geared herself up for a fight, and the fact that she didn't actually need to argue her case—that Dr Hamilton could make those same connections—made her feel suddenly weak at the knees. 'Thank you.'

'No, thank *you*. I didn't know about her kids having fractures, or it would've raised warning flags with me. The doctor who saw her this morning assumed the old breaks on the X-ray were because of...' He looked awkward. 'Well, domestic violence. We can't rule that out just yet, but we also need to confirm or rule out OI, so she gets the right treatment.'

'Absolutely.' Stephanie took a deep breath. 'Look, the children's ward has a liaison project running with the maternity unit, and it's really helping both of our departments. Maybe it's worth getting a few of the heads of department together and seeing if we can roll out the project between other departments, too.'

'To make sure we all have the information we need for our patients, you mean? Good idea.' Dr Hamilton smiled. 'I'll bring that one up at the departmental meeting next week and ask my head of department to talk to Rhys Morgan and Theo Petrakis.'

'Thanks. I, um, did say to Della that I'd see if I could have a word and get someone to bat for her.'

He nodded. 'I'll go and tell her what we're doing now.'

Insisting on being there wouldn't be fair; it would be interfering in another department, and Stephanie had no reason to doubt that Dr Hamilton would do his job properly. He certainly had a more open mind than the colleague who'd pigeonholed Della earlier. 'I haven't talked to her about a DEXA scan.'

'Don't worry. I'll explain what we're doing and reassure her,' Dr Hamilton promised.

'Thank you.'

Stephanie walked home, thinking about how ripped apart Della Goldblum was without her children. It was painfully close to how Stephanie herself felt about not having a family. She'd tried not to let it bother her, but deep down she knew it always had. Was there something unlovable about her? Why had she never managed to be part of a family?

And that made her question her feelings for Daniel. Did she want him because she wanted to be part of a family—exactly what he was offering her—or because she wanted him?

She had to be honest with herself and admit that it was both. But primarily she wanted Daniel. She wanted to be with him.

* * *

'Daddy, have you made it up with Stephanie yet?' Mia asked.

'We haven't fallen out,' Daniel replied, feeling guilty because he knew he was being economical with the truth. But it was complicated, and it was too much to expect a six-year-old to deal with.

'I miss her,' Mia said.

So did he. 'I'll see her soon, darling.'

'You could text her,' Mia persisted.

He smiled. 'Maybe later.' And not when his daughter was around. Because she'd want to know what Stephanie said, and he wanted to have enough time to work out how to deal with things.

He was halfway through cooking dinner when his phone beeped to signal an incoming text message.

Do you want to bring Thursday night forward?

She was ready to talk? Hope leaped in his veins.

Where and when?

Tonight. Mine. Dinner?

Oh, hell. He didn't want to knock Stephanie back, especially if she was going to tell him that she'd give his family a chance, but he couldn't just drop everything, either. He texted back.

Cooking dinner for Mia right now.

There was a long pause, and he thought maybe she'd backed off again, when his phone beeped.

Tomorrow night, if you can get a babysitter?

I'll be there. Half seven?

There was another long pause, and then another message:

Perfect.

Daniel was antsy all the next day. Dinner, she'd said. If she was going to call a halt to everything, she wouldn't suggest dinner, would she? Then again, how well did he know her?

His stomach was in knots by the time he rang her doorbell.

'Hi. Come up.' She buzzed him in and met him at her front door.

He handed her a bottle of wine. 'I wasn't sure whether to bring red or white, so I played it safe.'

She looked at the bottle. 'I love Chablis. Thank you—and it goes well with what I'm cooking. Actually, I should've asked—do you like fish?'

He smiled. 'Even if I didn't normally, I would tonight.'

She frowned at him. 'Dan, if you don't like fish, I can cook something else. There are other things in my fridge.'

'No, fish is fine.'

'And I'm being a bit lazy. It'll be literally five minutes until dinner.'

He raised an eyebrow. 'You're telling me you bought it from the supermarket?'

'No. I'm cooking. But fast food doesn't have to mean junk.'

'Says the foodie,' he teased.

For a moment, she thought he was going to kiss her. But he didn't. Had he changed his mind about her? No. She was being paranoid. He wouldn't be here if he didn't want to be. He was giving her space, not trying to bulldoze her.

And she loved him for it.

Her knees went weak as the thought registered. *She loved him*.

She busied herself with the food, just to stop herself thinking. Scallops in lime and chilli butter served with quinoa, steamed tenderstem broccoli and asparagus. She'd made pudding earlier: white chocolate mousse with raspberries. And although they chatted easily over dinner, both of them avoided the real issue.

Until she'd made coffee. Then Daniel asked, 'So are we going to talk about the elephant in the room?'

She took a deep breath. 'That's why I texted you yesterday. I was talking to a patient yesterday and it made me think about what I really want.'

He gave her a very intense look. 'What do you want, Stephanie?'

This was where she should come straight out with it. But fear made her check. 'Honestly?'

'Honestly.'

OK. She could do this. She could tell him. 'I want *you*. You, and Mia.' She dragged in a breath. 'But I'm so scared it's going to go wrong, Dan. I messed it up before. I can't afford to do the same again—there's not just you and me to think about. There's Mia. I don't want to hurt her.'

'I know. I want you, too,' he said. 'And it scares me just as much. I lost someone I loved very much and it was a random accident. There was nothing I could have done to stop that. But if I spend the rest of my life trying to wrap everyone I love in cotton wool, it'll drive me crazy and them even crazier. I just have to trust that lightning doesn't strike twice.' He paused. 'Actually, I might as well tell you the truth.'

'Truth?' Oh, help. Was he going to say now that he'd changed his mind?

'I love you, Stephanie.'

She stared at him, hope brimming over. 'You love me?'

'You make my world a better place,' he said simply. 'And I haven't been this happy in years.'

'Neither have I. And that scares me, too. How can I be sure that this is real—that it will last?'

'You can't. You just have to trust.'

'Which is a lot easier said than done,' she said dryly.

'I know. If it makes you feel any better, it scares me, too. Especially as I don't know how you feel about me.'

She hadn't told him? She stared at him in surprise. 'I love you, too, Dan.'

He came round to her side of the table then, and drew her into his arms. Kissed her. Yet it wasn't demanding; it was full of sweetness and tenderness. Giving, rather than taking.

She was shaking when he broke the kiss.

'What's wrong?' he asked softly.

'Too many mixed-up emotions in my head.' She swallowed hard. 'The biggest one being fear.'

'Of what?'

'Letting you down.' Just like she'd let Joe down.

'You're not going to let me down.'

'How do you know?'

'Because I trust you.' He stroked her face. 'I think you need to trust yourself, Stephanie. I know your ex's family pretty much trampled your confidence in yourself—but they were totally wrong about you. You trust yourself at work, don't you?'

'Of course I do. It's my job.'

'And you can bring exactly the same qualities to a family as you do to work,' he said softly. 'Kindness. Caring. Listening.'

She felt the tears well up. 'What if your family doesn't like me?'

'That's highly unlikely,' he said. 'Mia adores you. She's missed you.'

'I missed her, too.' She held his gaze. 'And you.'

'Good.'

'But what if the rest of your family doesn't feel the same way?' she persisted.

'Then we'll cross that bridge when we come to it. And there's really only one way to find out.'

Meet them. The thing she'd been holding back on. It didn't look as if she had a choice any more.

'What's going to be easier for you?' he asked. 'Meeting them all together, or keeping it small—say, meeting Lucy first, and then my parents?'

'Right at the moment, it's all one big, scary blur,' she admitted.

'OK. We'll tackle Lucy first. The next time we're both on a late, we'll meet her for coffee in her lunch break.' He kissed her lightly. 'It's all going to be fine. I promise you, my family's nice. And I don't break my promises.'

All she had to do was believe. Or at least *try*.

She took a deep breath. 'OK. Next time we're on a late. Friday morning?'

'That works for me.' He held her close. 'Thank you. I promise you won't regret it.'

She just hoped he was right.

CHAPTER THIRTEEN

THE NEXT MORNING, at work, Dr Hamilton called Stephanie about Della Goldblum's DEXA test.

'You were right. There are more X-rays and slight bowing of the long bones, some vertebral compressions, and her bone density is definitely not as good as it should be—her T-score is minus two.'

Stephanie had researched it and knew that meant Della's bone density was much lower than that of a normal, healthy person whose bone mass was at its peak; anything above minus one was fine, but anything below minus two was heading towards osteoporosis.

'I think you're right about the OI and we need to be really careful how we manage this,' he said. 'I don't want Della to be in pain, but I also don't want her immobilised with an epidural, so we'll need to look at a different form of pain management.'

'Thanks for letting me know,' Stephanie said. 'I'll set up a meeting with the social worker, because that's also going to affect the way the children are cared for. Obviously we still have to wait for the collagen results to prove that the children have it, too, but this is a pretty good indication of the way things will go.'

She'd stuck her neck out over this one, and she was so

glad she had. Della's family stood a real chance of being able to stick together and be happy.

Just before she was due in clinic, her phone shrilled again.

'Sorry, me again,' Dr Hamilton said. 'I know it's not your department, so strictly speaking I shouldn't even ask you this, but Della's asking if you'll be here while we talk about her condition. You're the only one she seems to trust.'

'Probably because I'm the only one who's listened to her, until you,' she said. 'Look, I have clinic now, but I'll come down on my break. Is it OK if I see you in a couple of hours?'

'That's great. Thanks.'

'Are you on duty tomorrow?' she asked.

'Yes.'

'It's my turn to be a bit cheeky,' she said. 'I have a meeting set up with the social worker tomorrow afternoon to discuss the children. Given that you're treating Della, it might help if you were there.'

'OK. I'll be there,' Dr Hamilton promised.

After clinic, Stephanie went over to the general surgical ward.

'Thanks for coming, Dr Scott,' Dr Hamilton said.

'We're colleagues, so I think we ought to be on first-name terms by now. I'm Stephanie.' She smiled at him.

'Ross.' He smiled back. 'Let's go and see Della.'

Della was lying in bed, clearly not feeling up to anything, but her face brightened when she saw Stephanie. 'You came.'

'Of course. Dr Hamilton here can explain a bit more about your condition than I can, but if you have any questions just ask,' Stephanie reassured her.

Ross Hamilton quickly explained about osteogenesis imperfecta. 'Basically it's a type of brittle bone disease and it's genetic, so your children have a fifty per cent chance of inheriting it from you.'

'Is it definite?'

'Not until we get the test results back,' Stephanie said. 'But, given they've both had fractures, my guess is that they have it, too.'

'If I'd known…' Della swallowed hard. 'I don't wish my kids away—of course I don't. I love them so much. But I hate myself for giving this to them.'

'You weren't to know,' Dr Hamilton said. 'It's only if you come to hospital to have a fracture treated and we do tests that you find out about the condition.'

Della bit her lip. 'So what does this mean for the kids? Can you cure it?'

'No, but we can manage it,' Dr Hamilton explained. 'As Stephanie said, at the moment we don't know for sure that they have it, but given that they've both had fractures it's a very strong possibility. We have to wait for the test results.'

'How long will that take?' Della asked.

'A few weeks, I'm afraid,' Stephanie said.

'Physiotherapy and exercise can help, and swimming's very good,' Dr Hamilton said. 'They might need surgery later; if they end up with a lot of fractures in their legs and arms, we can put a metal rod into the long bones to help manage that.'

'It's not going to affect their ability to think or to learn, and they can lead a pretty normal life with friends and a family,' Stephanie reassured her. 'We just need to try to minimise the risk of fractures.'

'And we can put you in touch with a support group,' Dr Hamilton added.

'It's pretty much business as usual, though you need to

be careful how you hold the baby and change him—I mean his clothes as well as his nappy,' Stephanie said.

Della looked anxious. 'The foster-parents need to know about this. I don't want him getting hurt.'

'We'll talk to them,' Stephanie promised. 'I have a meeting with social worker tomorrow so we can make sure they understand more about the condition, and Dr Hamilton is going to be there to back me up.'

Hope flared in Della's face. 'Does this mean they'll let me have the children back?'

The big question. Stephanie took a deep breath. 'Your diagnosis is proof that they were wrong about you. And I'll certainly bat for you.'

'Me, too,' Dr Hamilton said. 'We'll do our best for you, Della.'

'Thank you—both of you,' Della said. A tear trickled down her cheek. 'I thought I'd never get to see the kids again.'

'We're still not quite out of the woods,' Stephanie said. 'But we'll fight this to the top, if we have to.'

If only she had the same confidence about her personal life as she did about her private life, she thought wryly. Though that wasn't Della's problem, it was her own. And she needed to deal with it.

On Friday morning, on the way to meet Daniel's sister at the café, Stephanie felt physically sick. This was where it could all go wrong. Badly wrong.

Daniel laced his fingers through Stephanie's and squeezed gently. 'Stop worrying. This is going to be fine.'

'Uh-huh.' She knew he meant well, but she still couldn't stop the panic. Kitty hadn't liked her. What if Lucy didn't like her, either? She was pretty sure that Daniel was as close to Lucy as Joe had been to Kitty.

'Lucy knows you're worried about this and that you had a hard time with your ex's family,' Daniel said gently. 'Obviously I haven't told her any details—what you told me was in strict confidence and I won't break that—but I thought it only fair to let her know that there was something worrying you.'

'I guess so.' She took a deep breath.

He frowned. 'You're shaking.'

'I know I'm being a coward. This is way outside my comfort zone.'

'If you didn't know she was my sister—if you met her at a party or something—I think you'd become friends.'

Joe had been so sure that she'd be great friends with Kitty, and he'd been wrong. Was Dan just as blinkered where his sister was concerned? Or was she worrying over nothing?

'Let's go and sit down,' he said when they reached the café. 'I'll bring you a coffee.'

'Flat white, please.' If nothing else, it would give her something to do. Something to distract her from this horrible, horrible waiting. Something to distract her from the feeling of impending disaster.

Every time the door opened, Stephanie looked up, wondering if it was Lucy. But she was almost halfway through her coffee when a woman with the same dark hair and stunning blue eyes as Daniel walked in.

Daniel raised a hand in greeting, and Stephanie felt the adrenalin seep through to her fingertips. This was it.

The woman walked over to them, greeted Daniel with a hug, then held her hand out to Stephanie. 'Hi. I'm Lucy. Nice to meet you.'

Stephanie shook her hand. 'Nice to meet you, too.' It wasn't a total fib; she just didn't say that the whole thing terrified her. 'Can I get you a coffee?'

'Dan can do that.' She shooed her brother in the direction of the café's counter, then sat down at the table next to Stephanie. 'Thanks for agreeing to meet me. I know this must be pretty intimidating for you.'

'Dan told you about me.'

'Not much—but I'm in a similar situation. I've been seeing Jeff for a few weeks and we're getting to the point where we ought to introduce each other to the family, except I know his family really liked his ex, and it worries me they'll think I'm the only reason why Jeff and his ex aren't getting back together,' Lucy confided.

'Ouch, that's a tough one.'

'Mmm, particularly as he didn't tell them the real reason they broke up. He didn't want them to say anything about it accidentally in front of his son. You'd think that they'd work it out for themselves, given that Jeff has custody, but…' She grimaced. 'They blame him. Even though she was the one who had the affair and walked out.'

'That's hard on him—and on you.'

'Yeah.' Lucy took a deep breath. 'So hopefully, by me telling you that, you'll realise that I'm not going to judge you, because I'm secretly terrified of Jeff's family judging me too and deciding I'm not good enough.' She smiled at Stephanie. 'No doubt you're worrying about Meg, too. For what it's worth, yes, we all adored Meg, but it's not good for Dan to be alone. And I for one am glad he met you. It's nice to see him smile a bit more and look less lonely. Plus Mia told me all about you. As a primary school teacher, I know that kids tend to be good judges of character.'

The same, Stephanie knew, as being a paediatrician.

And then suddenly it was easy.

By the time Daniel came back with the coffees, Stephanie had relaxed enough to chat to Lucy, discovering they had shared tastes in books and music.

Finally, Lucy glanced at her watch. 'I have to be back at school. Stephanie, if we'd met for the first time at a book club or an exercise class, we would've become friends. I hope you can ignore the fact I'm Dan's sister and we can be friends.'

'Yes. I'd like that,' Stephanie said.

'Good.' Lucy hugged her. 'We'll do something girly together. Without Dan. I've got to rush back now, but get Dan to give you my number and call me. I mean it, Stephanie. Call me.'

'I will,' Stephanie promised, and meant it.

She and Daniel had time to linger for a bit longer until their shift was due to start.

'So was it as bad as you were expecting?' Daniel asked.

'No. She's nice,' Stephanie said. 'And you were right. If we'd met somewhere else and I didn't know she was your sister, we would've made friends.'

'She's not like your ex's sister?' he checked.

'No. I never had that kind of easiness with Kitty, not even in the few weeks when she did seem to soften a bit towards me.' She bit her lip. 'Actually, Dan, this does feel a bit too good to be true.'

'It isn't,' he said softly. 'Just believe. In yourself as well as in us.'

Could she take the risk? Could it really happen for her, this time, and she'd fit in?

On Friday afternoon, Ross Hamilton joined Stephanie for the meeting with the social worker. This time, to her relief, the social worker listened to their concerns and promised to talk to the foster-parents.

On her break, she visited Della. 'So has Dr Hamilton told you the good news?'

'They'll let me keep my kids?'

'The children will stay in care while you're in hospital,' Stephanie said. 'And if the tests show that the children have OI, then your case is proven and the children will be back with you.'

'Will the tests show it?' Della asked.

Stephanie smiled. 'I'm pretty sure they will.'

Daniel arranged to meet his parents for lunch in a nearby café, the following Tuesday.

'I know you're going to worry about this,' he said to Stephanie, 'but please give them a chance and don't assume they're going to be like your ex's family. Give it half an hour, and if you're still totally uncomfortable, I'll get you out of there. I'll do a fake call to you from the hospital so you can say you have to rush back, and I'll go with you, OK?'

'Thank you.' She gave him a rueful smile. 'I feel a bit pathetic. And mean, expecting you to give me a let-out like that.'

'It's understandable, given your past experience—but, remember, you got on fine with Lucy. You'll get on with my parents too.'

'Do they know?'

'That your in-laws have made you wary?' He nodded. 'I didn't go into detail. But I thought they needed to know why you're a bit antsy about meeting them.'

'Fair enough.' She squeezed his hand. 'I will try, Dan.'

'I know. And that's all I ask.'

Daniel's parents were already waiting for them in the café. Stephanie wasn't sure if she was relieved because it meant she wouldn't have to wait and worry or panicky because she still felt unprepared for this.

Daniel introduced them swiftly. 'Mum, Dad, this is

Stephanie. Stephanie, these are my parents, Hayley and Neville.'

'Pleased to meet you,' Stephanie said politely, and held her hand out to shake theirs in turn. Both had warm, firm handshakes. Please, please, let them be like their son, she thought.

Trying to ignore the rush of fear, she sat down.

'Dan, Nev, do you want to go and sort out the drinks?' Hayley asked with a smile.

Oh, help. This meant she was going to be on her own with Dan's mother. Then again, it had been fine when she'd been on her own with Lucy. She just had to trust Dan on this.

'Thanks for coming to meet us,' Hayley said.

Stephanie bit her lip. 'I'm sorry. You must think I'm really odd.'

'No. Dan obviously wouldn't break any confidences, but he did say that your in-laws were nightmares. Anyone would be wary after an experience like that.' Hayley smiled at her. 'I'm lucky. My mother-in-law was great. But my best friend's mother-in-law was a monster—she always made quite sure that she was the centre of attention. She would've tried the patience of a saint.'

'Ouch.' Stephanie looked at her. 'May I be honest with you?'

'Yes, of course.' Hayley looked slightly worried. 'What is it?'

'If you're uncomfortable with what I'm about to tell you, then tell me when I've finished and I'll back away from Dan.'

Hayley nodded. 'OK.'

Stephanie took a deep breath. 'Just to be clear, I'm not asking for sympathy. I'm just telling you the facts. I grew up in care. My mum was very young when she had me, and she found it hard to cope. The authorities took me away, but being without me was too much for her. Shortly after that she took her own life, leaving me parentless. And I guess I slipped through the net when it came to adoption. So I'm—well, not used to being in a family. I'm not very good at it.'

'Is that why your in-laws gave you a hard time?' Hayley asked.

'It wasn't all their fault. I can understand why. Of course they'd wonder what it was about me that had put people off.'

'More like you had a difficult start in life, and you've done remarkably well to get past that and train in such a caring profession. If I can be just as honest,' Hayley said, 'I think your in-laws needed a kick up the backside. They sound narrow-minded and petty, and you're well rid of them.'

Stephanie stared at her, not sure what to say. She really hadn't expected Hayley to come down so firmly on her side. Especially when they'd barely met.

Hayley reached over to squeeze her hand. 'You're the first woman Dan's dated since Meg was killed, and it's the first time I've seen the smile reach his eyes without being damped down by worry in a very, very long time. Mia never stops chatting about you. So, as far as I'm concerned, I'm more than happy to welcome you into his life. And I know Meg's parents feel the same way.'

That was even more shocking. Surely Meg's parents wouldn't want anyone taking their daughter's place? 'You've talked about it?' Stephanie asked, her voice scratchy with nerves.

'We're friends—and, yes, we've talked about it. We were worried about Dan because he'd pretty much shut himself away from the world. But we knew something was going on because he'd started to smile again and he's more relaxed with Mia. He's not so panicky that he's doing something wrong or that something's going to happen to Mia and he'll lose her, the same way he lost Meg.' Hayley squeezed Stephanie's hand again. 'And that's thanks to you. We owe you.'

'Of course you don't. I'm nothing special,' Stephanie said.

Hayley smiled. 'And the fact you can't see it for yourself…that makes you even more special, love.'

Unquestioning acceptance. Stephanie was almost too stunned to believe this was happening. She'd wanted it so badly from Joe's family, tried so hard, and got nowhere. Now it was being offered by Dan's family. Unconditionally.

Maybe she could have the family she'd always wanted. All she had to do was accept it.

Over lunch, Stephanie discovered that Neville was as warm and accepting as Hayley. He had a dry sense of humour and a nerdy streak that she really appreciated.

And when it was time to leave for the hospital, Daniel's parents hugged her warmly. 'I hope we'll see you again very soon,' Hayley said.

'I'd like that,' Stephanie said, hugging them back.

Daniel didn't say a word when they walked to the hospital. And she knew he was waiting for her to tell him what she thought.

In the end, she gave in. 'OK. You were right. They're lovely.'

He lifted both hands in a gesture of surrender. 'I'm not saying a word.'

'You're dying to say "I told you so", aren't you?' she teased.

'Well just a little bit.' His eyes crinkled at the corners. 'I'm glad you liked them. And they liked you.'

'I'm glad.'

He stood outside the hospital entrance. 'So does that mean we're officially an item now, Dr Scott?'

In answer, she reached up and kissed him. 'I don't care if the hospital grapevine talks about us. They'll soon find something else to talk about.'

Her reward was the brightest, brightest smile, and another kiss.

Katrina Morgan smiled at Stephanie as soon as she walked onto the ward. 'Hi, there. Are you OK to do the handover?'

'Sure,' Stephanie said, smiling back.

It didn't take long to go through the cases.

And then Katrina leaned back and folded her arms. 'I hear that a certain blue-eyed obstetrician has been seen with you.'

'Lunchtimes? That's to do with Rhys's pet project,' Stephanie said.

'I'm not sure Rhys gave you instructions to kiss the man silly outside the hospital entrance this afternoon.'

Stephanie felt her face flame. 'Um.'

Katrina just grinned and patted her hand. 'I'm teasing. Seriously, it's good that you and Dan are an item. He's a nice guy—and he's more than overdue a bit of sunshine in his life. As,' she added perceptively, 'I think you might be, too.'

'Maybe. It's early days.' Stephanie tried to play it down.

'Even so. You've looked happier lately. Now I know why. And I'm glad for both of you.'

CHAPTER FOURTEEN

OVER THE NEXT couple of weeks, Stephanie found herself growing closer to Daniel's family. Lucy talked her into going to a Pilates class with her, and Hayley met them both for a coffee afterwards.

'You should come with us, Mum,' Lucy said with a smile. 'It'd be really good for you.'

'I'll stick to walking the dog,' Hayley said. 'Right—bonfire night. Stephanie, we always have a bit of a party for Mia, with fireworks in the back garden and then food after. She's probably already badgered you about it, but will you come this year?'

'I, um—well, if you're sure.'

Hayley rolled her eyes. 'Love, I wouldn't ask you if I didn't want you there. Are you on duty, or can you swap?'

'Is that Bonfire Night itself, or the nearest Saturday?' Stephanie asked.

'Bonfire Night. I'm doing pulled pork this year, with Boston beans and jacket potatoes.'

'Can I bring something?' Stephanie asked. 'I have this great recipe for toffee-apple cookies. I've promised Mia for ages that we'll make them together.'

'Perfect,' Hayley said with a smile. 'Dan will pick you up.'

'And you'll get to meet Jeff,' Lucy said. 'He's bringing Mikey.'

Hayley looked slightly awkward. 'I normally invite Meg's parents, too. Will you be all right with that?'

'That's fine,' Stephanie fibbed.

'They're looking forward to meeting you,' Hayley said, and squeezed her hand. 'They know we like you, and I promise it's not going to be difficult for anyone.'

To Stephanie's surprise, she discovered that the Parkers were just as welcoming as the Connors. And she enjoyed herself hugely at the party, holding Mia's hand while the men took turns in lighting the fireworks, and joining Hayley, Lucy and Hestia in the kitchen to help serve the food.

'Those cookies are awesome,' Lucy said after the first mouthful. 'Next school fundraiser, I'm *so* going to be begging you to make these for us.'

'Any time,' Stephanie said, meaning it.

'So was it OK?' Daniel asked afterwards, when Mia was tucked up in bed and Stephanie was sharing a glass of wine with him.

'More than OK. Obviously I've been to bonfire parties before, but they've always been work things. I've never done the fireworks in the back garden thing. And I loved it.' She smiled at him. 'Meg's parents were nice. I can't believe they were so sweet to me.'

'The Parkers are lovely,' he said. 'Actually, Hestia had a quiet word with me when I was helping with the dishes. She said she approves of you, and thinks Meg would've liked you a lot.'

Stephanie had to blink tears away. 'I still wonder if I'm going to pinch myself and wake up. This is almost too good to be true.'

He leaned over and kissed her. 'Believe me, it's real all right.'

By the middle of November, Christmas preparations were everywhere; the lights in Oxford Street had been turned on and the shops were full of tinsel and presents. Every ward in the hospital had made arrangements for bran-tub Christmas presents, and the children's ward had organised Rhys to come in on Christmas morning as Santa, to deliver presents from the Friends of the London Victoria for the in-patient children and their brothers and sisters.

Was this Christmas going to be her first truly happy Christmas? Stephanie wondered.

'What are you doing for Christmas?' Daniel asked.

'I'm on duty,' she said. She'd slipped into the habit fairly soon after marrying Joe, as a way out of spending the day with his family. 'What about you?'

'I'm going over to Mum and Dad's with Mia,' he said. 'If you'd like to join us, that'd be lovely.'

'Thanks, but, um…'

He sighed. 'I was hoping you felt more comfortable around my family now.'

'I know—and I honestly am.' And she knew it was ridiculous to fear that Christmas would be when everything changed—when she found out that she didn't really fit in after all, and it really was too good to be true.

'OK. I won't nag,' he said, and she was relieved to change the subject.

Until she had lunch with Lucy and Hayley.

'So are you coming to us for Christmas?' Hayley asked.

Oh, help. 'Dan said something, didn't he?' she asked.

'Well—yes,' Hayley admitted. 'I have to admit, I just assumed that you'd be coming. We'd love you to be with us at Christmas.'

'But, just in case you think we're just being nice,' Lucy said, 'we do have an ulterior motive.'

'Which is?'

Lucy gave her a hug. 'Don't look so worried. I'm teasing.'

As usual, Stephanie had misread the cues. Why couldn't she get it right?

'Well, ish,' Lucy continued. 'We've heard that you're the departmental quiz queen, and we really want you on our Trivial Pursuit side so Dan and Dad have to eat humble pie for the first year ever. So you have to come for Christmas. We need you. Desperately.'

'You're really sure about this?' Stephanie asked.

'Really,' Hayley assured her.

'Jeff and Mikey are coming,' Lucy added, 'so you won't be the only one there for the first time.'

'It's really kind of you to invite me, but I'm working on Christmas Day,' Stephanie said. 'I thought it was only fair to let the people with children spend the day with them.'

'That's not a problem,' Hayley said. 'We can have Christmas dinner in the evening instead of at lunchtime.'

Stephanie looked at her, horrified. 'You don't have to change things for me.'

Lucy punched her arm. 'Steffie, have you ever considered that we might want to?'

'Oh—well, no,' Stephanie admitted.

'Are we railroading you?' Lucy asked.

Stephanie wrinkled her nose. 'I'm not very good with families.'

'You are with ours,' Hayley reminded her. 'What's really worrying you?'

She sighed. 'There were strict traditions at Joe's parents' house.'

'Such as?' Hayley asked.

'When you were allowed to open presents, what you had to eat and when—and they always ended up in a kind of huddle round the sofa, talking about Christmases past.'

'Excluding you?' Lucy asked perceptively.

'I don't think they meant to, exactly,' Stephanie said, trying hard to be fair. 'It was just how it was.'

'Well, it's not like that in our house,' Hayley said. 'Yes,

there are some things we do traditionally but traditions are supposed to grow and change with you.'

Stephanie gave a noncommittal murmur.

'Your ex-in-laws have a lot to answer for,' Hayley said dryly. 'Well, you're part of us now, and we want you there for Christmas. It won't be the same without you.'

Stephanie knew when she was beaten. 'Is there anything I can do to help?'

'No, just be there,' Hayley said.

'Though, if you want to make cookies, we won't say no,' Lucy added.

'Cookies it is,' Stephanie said. 'And Mia can help. She loves baking.'

'Daddy's sad,' Mia confided to Stephanie. 'He's always sad today.'

'Why?' Stephanie asked carefully.

'Because it's Mummy's anniversary. He always takes her flowers today. And that's why Auntie Lucy was supposed to bring me home from school. 'Cept she had a 'mergency meeting, and Nanna Parker's sad today, and Nanna Connor's visiting her sister in Scotland…'

'And that's why Lucy rang me to see if I could pick you up?' Stephanie said.

Mia nodded. 'Will you help me make Daddy smile?'

Stephanie sat down and scooped the little girl onto her lap. 'I'll try. But sometimes you can't help being sad when you miss someone, and today's the day he'll miss your mum.'

'I don't really remember her now,' Mia said. 'But I know what she looks like, because we have photos. Lots of photos.'

'That's good,' Stephanie said, a lump forming in her throat.

'Do you have a day when you miss your mum?' Mia asked.

'I do,' Stephanie said. 'I take her flowers, just like your dad takes your mum flowers. It's in April, when the daffodils are out.'

'I like daffodils,' Mia said. 'Yellow flowers are happy flowers.' She frowned. 'But they won't make Daddy happy.'

'We could make him something special for tea,' Stephanie said. 'A pizza with a smiley face on it.'

'Brilliant,' Mia said. 'And you make him happy. He smiles a lot more.' She hugged Stephanie. 'You make me happy, too.'

Stephanie had to blink back the tears.

'Are you crying?' Mia asked, looking shocked.

'Happy tears,' Stephanie said. 'Because you and your dad make me happy, too.'

She spent a while making a pizza from scratch with Mia and letting the little girl decorate it. And she quietly texted Daniel to let him know that she was looking after Mia and he wasn't to worry about anything; she'd stay as long as he was needed.

Daniel turned up half an hour later, when Mia had had a bath and talked Stephanie into reading three stories to her.

He hugged her. 'Thanks for being here.'

'Any time.' And she meant it. She'd loved every second of looking after Mia. And today had shown her that she really could connect with the little girl, be there for her when she was sad and explain things to her so she felt better. That maybe, just maybe, she could be the mother Mia clearly wanted.

Daniel made the effort to be excited about Mia's smiley-face pizza, and when Mia was in bed—after three more stories read by Stephanie—he poured them both a glass of wine.

'Are you sure you don't want me to go?' she asked. 'I know what today is.'

'I'm sure.' He held her close. 'Knowing I was coming home to you and Mia—that made a real difference to me. It's made today less bleak. It still hurts, but I'm finally healing. And that's all thanks to you.'

She stroked his face. 'Hardly. I come with just as much baggage.'

'I hate this time of year,' he said. 'And I guess it's the same for you.'

'When you have to be all smiley-smiley because it's Christmas, and everyone's getting excited about parties, and all my patients are getting excited about Father Christmas…' She nodded. 'But it's not quite as hard this year. Thanks to you and Mia.'

'I can never face decorating the house until after today,' Daniel said. 'It doesn't feel right doing it before then. But this weekend Mia and I always go to choose a tree. Come with us?'

Choose a tree. Something she'd never, ever done—because Joe had always insisted on having an artificial tree rather than a real one. A tree that wouldn't shed needles or look scruffy at any point. And he'd insisted on keeping the tree he'd bought the year before he'd met her, so she'd had no part in choosing a tree or any kind of decorations.

'I'd like that,' she said. 'Very much.'

On the Saturday morning, Stephanie went with Mia and Daniel to choose a Christmas tree, then spent the afternoon at their house, helping to decorate it.

'Have you already decorated your tree? 'Mia asked.

'Um, no—I don't have one,' Stephanie admitted.

Mia frowned. 'Why not?'

Oh, help. She didn't want to upset the little girl with the real reason: she hadn't bothered with one since the divorce because it had seemed pointless having a Christmas tree just for one. 'I haven't had time to buy one,' she hedged.

'We could help you buy one,' Mia said, looking hopeful.

'I...' She gave in. 'OK.'

'Tomorrow?'

'If your dad doesn't already have plans.'

Daniel came back in to overhear the last bit. 'Plans for what?'

'Finding a Christmas tree for Stephanie,' Mia said.

He smiled. 'That's fair enough. You helped us with ours.'

Mia hugged her. 'That's settled, then.'

Stephanie couldn't help smiling; she could hear Lucy and Hayley so clearly in Mia's voice. 'It's settled,' she agreed.

Mia was thrilled to help choose not only the tree but the decorations, too. They spent half the afternoon putting the decorations on the tree, and Stephanie lifted her up so she could put the angel on the very top.

'You've done a fantastic job. Thank you so much,' Stephanie said, and kissed the tip of Mia's nose.

Mia stared at her, then put her arms round Stephanie's neck. 'You kissed me.'

'Is that OK?' Had she gone too far?

Mia nodded. 'But you only kiss people you love.'

'Ye-es.'

'I love you,' Mia said, and kissed the end of Stephanie's nose.

And Stephanie had a huge lump in her throat as she whispered, 'I love you, too.'

The little girl fell asleep on the sofa not long afterwards, clearly tired out. Stephanie gently put a blanket over her.

'I ought to get her home,' Daniel said.

Stephanie shook her head. 'Don't wake her just yet,

Dan.' She paused. 'Well, now I have a tree, I really ought to have a Christmas party.'

'The three of us?' he asked.

'I was thinking, is it too late to ask your family over for Christmas Eve?'

'That's a great idea,' Dan said. 'Call them.'

'What, now?'

He smiled. 'Yes, now.'

By the time she'd ended the call, he was smiling. 'I think half of London must've heard the shrieks of glee from Mum and Lucy.'

'It's only a party,' Stephanie said lightly. 'A simple buffet. Lucy's bringing a pudding, and your mum's bringing chocolates to go with the coffee.'

He looked slightly worried. 'Are they taking over?'

'No,' she said softly. 'They want to feel part of it. And they want me to feel that I'm—well, part of the family.'

'You *are* part of the family.' He kissed her lightly. 'And I'm proud of you. That must've been hard.'

'Baby steps,' Stephanie said. And, with Daniel and Mia by her side, they were easier than she could ever have imagined.

CHAPTER FIFTEEN

A FEW DAYS later, Daniel and Stephanie took Mia to see Father Christmas.

'Now, young lady, what do you want Father Christmas to bring you this year?' he asked.

The little girl beckoned him closer. 'I want a mummy for Christmas,' she whispered.

'But isn't that your mummy and daddy there?' he whispered back.

'No, just my daddy. My mummy's in heaven.'

'But you'd like someone to be your mummy?'

'I want Stephanie,' she said simply. 'Daddy loves her and so do I. I know she loves me. I just want her to love Daddy, too, and get married.'

'I'll see what I can do,' Father Christmas said. 'For now, my elves made this especially for you.' He handed her a parcel. 'Merry Christmas. Ho, ho, ho.'

'Merry Christmas, Santa,' Mia said.

But when Mia joined Daniel and Stephanie, Father Christmas beckoned Stephanie to him. 'Can I have a quick word?' he asked.

She stared at him, surprised. 'Sure. Daniel, I'll catch you and Mia up in a second, OK?' She turned to Father Christmas. 'Is something the matter?'

'Not exactly.' He sighed. 'I'm not supposed to do this—

but it's Christmas and I've got a daughter a couple of years younger than your little one. And if this is my chance to do a real Santa thing and give someone the present they most want in the world, I'm taking it.'

Stephanie blinked. 'What did she ask you for?'

'A mummy for Christmas,' he said.

'Oh.' Her breath caught. 'That's what she said?'

'She says her dad loves you and so does she. She just wants you to love her dad and get married.'

Stephanie blew out a breath. 'For Christmas. Right.'

'Sorry if I've spoken out of turn. I didn't mean to offend. But—well, what she said touched my heart.'

Stephanie smiled at him. 'You haven't offended me at all. And thank you. Now I know what she's thinking. And her dad and I definitely need to talk about this when she's asleep.'

'Good luck,' he said. 'And Merry Christmas.'

'You, too,' she said.

'So what did you want to talk to me about?' Daniel asked, once Mia was asleep.

'Father Christmas,' she said.

He frowned. 'I'm not with you.'

'Mia told him what she wanted.' She paused. 'She wants a mummy for Christmas.'

He grimaced. 'One of her friends just got a new stepmum. Don't feel pressured. It's probably a phase.'

'No. She, um, wants me,' Stephanie said softly, and told him what Father Christmas had told her. 'I think she's accepted me, Dan.'

'More than accepted, I'd say. She loves you. My whole family loves you,' he said.

And the fact that she'd told him all this instead of keeping it to herself gave him hope. Maybe now she was ready to put the past behind her. 'And she's right. I love you.' He stroked her face, 'I probably should wait and do this in a much more romantic place than my living room, but…' He dropped to one knee. 'Stephanie, you make me happy and you make my daughter happy, too—will you marry us?'

Her eyes filled with tears, and he knew she wasn't going to say yes.

'I need to think about it, Dan,' she said quietly.

Because she was still worried it would all go wrong?

He wondered if he was ever going to be able to help her over that last hurdle. He could believe in them and trust that they would stay together and she wouldn't be taken from him like Meg was. So why couldn't she trust that he wouldn't put her last, the way her ex had?

'OK. Think about it,' he said. 'But know that I love you, Mia loves you, and we're not giving up on you any time soon.'

Stephanie thought about it.

And thought some more.

And thought about it even more on the train back to Manchester, where she'd arranged to visit Trish to swap Christmas presents.

Trish met her at the station with a warm hug, and drove them back to her house. But it wasn't until Calum had an afternoon nap that Stephanie finally spilled the beans.

'Dan asked me to marry him.'

'What? That's fantastic!' Trish whooped. 'I get to be maid of honour, right?'

'I haven't said yes.'

'Why? Are you insane?' Trish asked. 'All right. Let's take this slowly. Dan loves you and wants you to marry him. Mia wants you to be her mum. Yes?'

'Yes.'

'Is that what you want?'

Stephanie bit her lip and nodded.

Trish hugged her. 'Steffie, you have to let the past go. From what you've told me about Dan's family, they're lovely. They're nothing like Joe's lot.'

'I know,' Stephanie said in a small voice. 'But there's just something inside me that panics.'

'You think that because your mum had to give you up and you were never adopted, there's something wrong with you—that you're not lovable?' Trish asked softly.

'It's crossed my mind a couple of times,' Stephanie admitted.

'More like, you've been brooding about it. You idiot.' Trish hugged her again. 'You really need to talk more and worry less. Your mum loved you, but she was too young to cope. Her parents—well, they weren't real parents, were they? All they thought about was their social standing, and they would've made you unhappy.'

'I know that.'

'And as for Joe—nobody would've been good enough for him, in his parents' eyes. And Joe himself didn't have the backbone to stand up for you when he should've done.' She paused. 'What would Dan have done, in his shoes?'

'Stood up for me,' Stephanie said. 'But he wouldn't have been in that situation, because his family like me.'

'Like you?' Trish pushed.

'Love me.' Stephanie sighed. 'And I love them. I love Mia. I love Dan.'

'All you have to do is say yes. That's what you want isn't it?'

Stephanie nodded. 'But I've given Dan such a hard time. He's opened himself up despite losing his first wife in such tragic circumstances. And I've pushed him away. I've let the past get in the way.'

'So make it up to him,' Trish said with a grin. 'Are you seeing him tonight, when you get back to London?'

'No. It'll be late when I get back.'

'Doesn't matter. Surprise him,' Trish said.

Stephanie thought about it all the way home on the train. *Surprise him.*

Yes, she could do that. Prove to him that she believed in him and she believed in their future. But she'd need a teensy little bit of help.

She grabbed her mobile phone and called Lucy. 'I need to meet you and your mum for a drink,' she said.

'Why?'

'Because I need to talk to you about something—oh, and please don't breathe a word to Dan.'

'This,' Lucy said, 'sounds like a plot. I'm intrigued. OK. The wine bar round the corner from my flat, tomorrow at seven. We'll be there waiting for you.'

'Thanks, Lucy. I really appreciate it.'

Just as Lucy had promised, she and Hayley were at the wine bar. They waved to Stephanie as soon as she walked in.

'Don't keep us in suspense any longer,' Lucy begged.

'OK.' Stephanie told them about Father Christmas. 'And Dan asked me to marry him,' she finished.

Lucy hugged her. 'Fantastic—I get a sister!'

Hayley hugged her, too. 'And I get another daughter. I'm so pleased for you both, sweetheart.'

Stephanie bit her lip. 'I feel like the meanest woman on the planet. I, um, haven't said yes.'

Lucy looked shocked. 'Why not?'

Stephanie took a deep breath. 'Because I'm stupid and stubborn and scared.'

'Do you love him?' Hayley asked.

'I do. I asked him to give me some time to think about

it. But I really think I need to show some faith in him. I need to show him what he means to me. And I was thinking about it all the way home from Manchester yesterday.' She outlined her plan. 'Do you think that would work?'

'That's just lovely,' Lucy said. 'And I think Mia could keep a secret this big. You're going to tell her, right?'

'She's going to be my wing woman on this—well, wing girl,' Stephanie said. 'And you're both sworn to secrecy.'

'More secrets,' Hayley grumbled, but she was smiling. 'This is going to be the best Christmas ever.'

'Why can't I come in?' Daniel asked plaintively in the kitchen doorway on Christmas Eve.

'Because this is woman's work,' Mia said, with her hands on her hips. 'And you're not a girl.'

Stephanie just about managed to stop herself laughing. 'I'll bring you a cup of tea and a sandwich,' she promised. 'But Mia's right. You have to stay out of the kitchen.'

Mia gave her a high five. 'He won't be cross any more when he sees them,' she said in a stage whisper, indicating the cupcakes that they'd been decorating together.

They finished decorating the cakes and arranged them carefully on a platter. Then Stephanie covered them, just in case Daniel decided to sneak into the kitchen. She didn't want him seeing them until she was ready.

'You,' she said to Mia, 'are the best helper ever.'

'And you,' Mia said, 'are a brilliant cook. We're a good team.'

They were, Stephanie thought. And that included Dan.

She helped Mia get ready in a pretty party dress, and painted her nails the same colour as Mia's.

'That's perfect,' Mia said with a broad smile.

Daniel was kept busy answering the door and letting

everyone up to the flat. And when everyone was there, Mia said, 'It's time.'

'Time for what?' Daniel asked.

'Stephanie's got something to ask you,' Mia said importantly.

He frowned. 'What?'

Together, Stephanie and Mia lifted the cover from the cakes. 'Dan, you need to read this,' Stephanie said softly. 'And this is why we wouldn't let you in the kitchen this afternoon.'

He read the message iced onto the cupcakes—a different letter on each one.

Will you marry me?

The lump in his throat was so big that he couldn't speak at first. He could hardly believe that she'd done this. It was a public declaration of love, in front of all the people closest to him. He'd been so sure that she'd be too scared to accept his proposal; since she'd asked him for time to think about it, he'd backed off.

And now she was asking him.

'I asked you first,' he said shakily. 'You're not supposed to answer a question with another question.'

She smiled. 'That's my answer. I love you, Daniel Connor.'

And all the shadows, all the fear in her eyes, had gone. 'I love you, too.' He wrapped her in his arms. 'Yes. I'll be proud to marry you, Stephanie Scott.'

'And I'll be your flower girl,' Mia piped up, 'with Aunty Lucy and Stephanie's best friend Trish as your bridesmaids.'

Clearly, Dan thought, Mia and Stephanie had been discussing this. They'd probably even started planning colours and dresses and flowers.

His girls.

His family.

Lucy said, 'I think this calls for champagne.'

'Funnily enough,' Hayley said, 'we brought some.'

The smiles on their faces told him that they'd known all about this, too. Stephanie had been confident enough to let them in on her plans. Accepted them as her family. Taken her place, right in the middle of everyone.

'Santa's given me what I really wanted,' said Mia. 'A mummy for Christmas.'

Stephanie smiled. 'And I get what I really want, too. All I've ever wanted. A family of my own. The best family in the world…'

* * * * *

A sneaky peek at next month...

Medical Romance

CAPTIVATING MEDICAL DRAMA—WITH HEART

My wish list for next month's titles...

In stores from 6th December 2013:

☐ From Venice with Love – Alison Roberts

& Christmas with Her Ex – Fiona McArthur

☐ After the Christmas Party... – Janice Lynn

& Her Mistletoe Wish – Lucy Clark

☐ Date with a Surgeon Prince – Meredith Webber

& Once Upon a Christmas Night... – Annie Claydon

Available at WHSmith, Tesco, Asda, Eason, Amazon and Apple

Just can't wait?

Visit us Online

You can buy our books online a month before they hit the shops! **www.millsandboon.co.uk**

1113/03

Special Offers

Every month we put together collections and longer reads written by your favourite authors.

Here are some of next month's highlights— and don't miss our fabulous discount online!

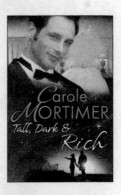

On sale 6th December

On sale 1st November

On sale 6th December

Save 20%
on all Special Releases

Doctors, romance, passion and drama—in the city that never sleeps

Available as a bundle at
www.millsandboon.co.uk/medical

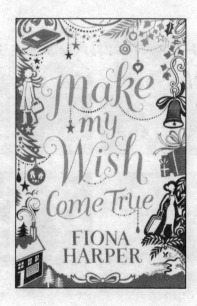

Wrap up warm this winter with Sarah Morgan...

Sleigh Bells in the Snow

Kayla Green loves business and hates Christmas.

So when Jackson O'Neil invites her to Snow Crystal Resort to discuss their business proposal… the last thing she's expecting is to stay for Christmas dinner. As the snowflakes continue to fall, will the woman who doesn't believe in the magic of Christmas finally fall under its spell…?

4th October

www.millsandboon.co.uk/sarahmorgan

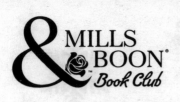